Also by M.T. Bass

My Brother's Keeper

Crossroads

In the Black

Lodging

Somethin' for Nothin'

Untethered

Murder by Munchausen

THE DARKNET

MURDER BY MUNCHAUSEN BOOK #2

BY

M.T. BASS

AN ELECTRON ALLEY PUBLICATION

MUDCAT FALLS, U.S.A.

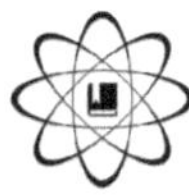

Electron Alley Corporation
The Herald Building
732 Broadway Avenue
Lorain, OH 44052

This book is a work of fiction. Any references to historical events, real people, or real places are used fictitiously. Other names, characters, places and events are products of the author's imagination and any resemblance to actual events or places or persons living or dead is entirely coincidental.

Manufactured in the United States of America

Edited by Elizabeth Love (www.bee-edited.com)

ISBN 978-1-946266-03-3 (Trade Paperback)
ISBN 978-1-946266-04-0 (Pocket Paperback)
ISBN 978-1-946266-02-6 (eBook)

www.MTBass.net

For Karen

The Three Laws

1. A civilian-owned and operated synthetic humanoid entity may not act in any manner so as to engage in or cause any harmful or offensive contact against a human being or, through inaction, allow a human being to come to harm.

2. A civilian-owned and operated synthetic humanoid entity must obey the directives and orders given it by human beings except in those instances where such directives and orders would conflict with the First Law.

3. A civilian-owned and operated synthetic humanoid entity may protect its own existence as long as such protection does not conflict with the First or Second Laws.

Federal Technology Administration Regulations

*Our technology, our machines, is part of our humanity.
We created them to extend ourselves, and that is what
is unique about human beings.*

~Ray Kurzweil

The Baron

Jake crossed beneath the crime scene tape and walked towards me as I stood guard over the covered body holding the bunny suit crew at bay from their forensic harvest. He does have the best poker face of anyone I know, but—ugh! I could practically smell it on him: the blonde waitress from John's.

I nodded to the Medical Examiner to pull back the sheet from the body. "Looks like your case is closed, too."

Jake peered down at Jeffery's corpse on the pavement. "But…he didn't do that to himself."

I gazed up overhead at the fat, heavy clouds glowing gray from the city lights. "You don't have to say it, but you will, won't you. You can't help yourself."

He stared at the eviscerated body that was the subject of an arrest warrant in his Munchausen murder with its intestines wrapped around the neck like a fine silk tie.

"What did you call him? The Baron?"

Jake just nodded.

"I guess he's still out there."

"Yeah…in the Darknet."

"Huh?"

Just then Lt. Sands came up behind us. "Well, this looks like nothing but trouble."

I had called him, too.

"What? Me or the dead body?" Jake asked with a smirk.

"Dead bodies are easy." Sands put his hand on Jake's shoulder. "They don't break any regs, and they don't smart off."

"Hi, Lieu. I thought you should know, too."

"But he got here before me." He squeezed Jake's shoulder hard.

"Well, maybe he didn't have anything better to do at the moment," I said, staring Jake down. Still, the best poker face ever.

"You know how it is." Jake gave Lt. Sands a fake wince, then winked. "Most people call 911. I *am* 911."

Lt. Sands rolled his eyes and shook his head. "So, what am I looking at, Maddie?"

"No doubt, a big fat 'I told you so' coming our way, courtesy of the Geek Squad here," I said.

"We need to get started," whined one of the Bunny Suit Boys behind us. "Before it rains again or we'll lose evidence."

We backed off, and I waved them forward to process the crime scene.

"You know what this means, right?" Lt. Sands asked us as we huddled apart from the crowd of technicians.

I looked at Jake.

He smiled that crooked, knowing smile of his. "Partners again, huh."

I clenched my eyes shut and shook my head. *Damn it.*

"Well, you kids have fun. I'm going back to bed." Lt. Sands could barely suppress his chuckling. He turned to leave. "Tomorrow afternoon. In my office. We'll talk. You detectives have a good night—well, morning, now."

I opened my eyes and caught Jake laughing.

The Darknet

"Come on. It won't be that bad, will it?"

I pushed past Jake to supervise *my* crime scene.

Of course, it wasn't that Jake was a bad cop or difficult to work with. When we were *professional* partners, we made a good team. Just now…

I suddenly caught movement out of the side of my eye. Rapid footsteps hit the wet pavement. Jake ran by me, and before I even thought about it, I instinctively took off after him like a partner would.

In the dim glow of tired, old street lamps, a short figure fled up the sidewalk ahead of Jake. I slipped between two parked cars to cross the street so I could cut him off if he veered to the left.

No thinking. Just running.

Another block and our runner instinctively paused as if to look both ways for traffic at the deserted intersection. Jake closed the gap between them quickly.

The perp looked over his shoulder and bolted quickly my way, caught sight of me, and zig-zagged back the other way right into Jake's path.

Instead of tackling, Jake grabbed his collar like the scruff of a dog's neck, and they twirled in a weird, contorted ballroom dance kind of way around and around and around until they tumbled into a heap on the pavement.

I crossed back over and drew down with my Glock…*on a kid*. So young I couldn't tell at first if it was a boy or a girl, especially dressed street-person style in layers of grimy tattered clothes.

Jake scrambled to his feet and held the kid by the collar like a trophy-sized walleye. He panted, "I think we just might have a witness."

I shot him a look, holstered my weapon and knelt down to eye-level just out of a pre-teen's arm reach. I saw by the eyes and soft facial features it was a young girl. "Are you okay?"

The kid shrugged and wriggled futilely in Jake's grasp.

"Hey, settle down," Jake commanded, with a shake of the girl's collar.

Our eyes met again. I always liked how he and I were on the same wavelength. Almost like ESP, we were instinctively working the kid Good Cop/Bad Cop. I missed it. It wasn't there with Walker, who took Jake's place when he got suspended for shooting the Councilman's son or now with Sanchez who was still back at the crime scene. I couldn't even begin to imagine her chasing a perp down the street. And what would the point be? She's a good cop and all but probably runs a four-hour mile—or maybe "waddles" would be more accurate.

"Hungry?"

No response, except in the eyes.

"Yeah. Let's see what we've got."

We led the kid back towards the crime scene but stayed well outside the tape. Jake took her to my unmarked car and sat her in the back seat—Sanchez would be sure to gripe about the body odor.

"Don't make me cuff you." Jake made his point with a poke to the shoulder but stood blocking her escape path.

"I'll be right back." I smiled, looked towards Jake, and rolled my eyes for the kid's benefit.

On my way to the food and coffee, I instructed a patrolman to discretely circle around and stand guard down the street and out of sight from the sedan in case the kid tried to take off again.

The Darknet

I grabbed a couple of donuts and a bottled water.

"Whatcha got going on over there?" Sanchez asked, slapping her notepad against her ample thigh like an impatient meter maid.

"I don't know. Some kid who bolted out of the alley, there. Might have seen something. Maybe."

"I'll call Protective Services."

"Yeah, but maybe give me a few minutes head start with her to see if there's any there, there."

"I wouldn't worry about that. I haven't met a social worker yet who likes coming out in the middle of the night."

"Thanks."

"Good thing you called him."

"Huh?"

"Jake." Sanchez smiled. "Foot races ain't my thing. I don't think I've actually run since the academy."

"Yeah. At least he's good for something." I smiled back.

"Whatever you say, honey." Sanchez laughed out loud. "I'll see if I can light a fire under Forensics so we can get out of here before morning rush hour."

When I got back, Jake drifted away from the sedan to give us some space. Kneeling again, I offered up the donuts. The kid grabbed them both and ate the first one with a fierce animal intensity, then seemed to remember her manners and took a dainty bite out of the second one.

"Thanks."

I nodded. "You know the drill, right? We have to call them."

The kid gave a heavy sigh and washed a bite down with a sip of water.

"You have to?" she whispered.

I nodded. "What name will you give them?"

"Um, Amy, I guess."

I had to grit my teeth hard to keep from screaming. "Anywhere close to your real name?"

She shook her head. "Why?"

"In case I want to check in on you."

"I won't be there long. Never am. And they never come after me."

"Did you see what happened?" I motioned towards the taped off crime scene with my head, then looked at Jake who hovered just out of ear shot over on the sidewalk. "Trust me, he won't let it rest and can make life miserable if you let him."

Amy looked at Jake, then back to me. "It was one of them."

"Them?"

"You know. A robot."

"How could you tell?" I had a hard time picking them out myself.

"Not many of 'em down here under the bridges. They kind of stick out."

I sighed. *The Baron.*

"Yeah. I hate them, too," Amy said, then finished off the second donut.

~~~

Throwing Lead

It can be therapeutic, especially early in the morning when the Department range is typically a ghost town. SWAT won't mob the place until at least mid-morning, and most guys worried about qualifications don't come in until later in the afternoon—before or after their tour. There are only a few of us who come regularly to hone our shooting skills, something ingrained in me by my dad.

From outside, I heard the familiar rhythm of his drill as he drew, fired, and holstered his gun, then drew again: *Tap…Tap-tap…………Tap…Tap-tap……*

Unfortunately, one of the us's is Jake.

He was in a far stall, so I took one near the door, put up a target and went to work. I don't know how long it had been because I cleared my mind and tuned out the world as bullets shredded cardboard, but suddenly the range was empty except for me. Pushing cartridges into empty magazines, my skin began to tingle like spiders were crawling all over me. He was still there. Outside, watching me through the window. But I didn't turn around. I reloaded and focused on the silhouette of a man fifty feet away. The chill went away as I threw lead downrange.

When I got upstairs, Jake was there making small talk with Lt. Sands in his office. While they joked and laughed, I went through my morning nesting routine at my desk, then filled a cup with coffee.

Boys, they're all the same. They get that sheepish, hand-in-the-cookie-jar look whenever we interrupt them, no matter who they are or what they're doing.

"Maddie, come on in." Lt. Sands motioned me into his office at my knock.

Jake turned and smiled. "Mornin', Mads."

I acknowledged with a tip of my cup and a sip of coffee, then Jake and I sat down in the chairs in front of Lt. Sands' desk like two kids called down to the principal's office.

"Where's Sanchez?" I asked. "Shouldn't she be here, too?"

"Haven't seen her yet," Sands said, scanning the squad room over our shoulders. He called down to the desk sergeant.

I felt Jake staring at me but wouldn't give him the satisfaction.

"Saw you down on the range this morning," he finally said.

I turned and smiled slyly. "You want me to keep sharp, don't you? We wouldn't want an errant round causing a blue-on-blue incident."

Jake smiled. "Yeah. Think of the paperwork."

"Detective. Come on in," Sands greeted Sanchez. He gave me and Jake the hairy eyeball. "Maddie and Jake were just catching up on old times."

Sanchez looked at us like scolded children and shook her head. She sat down on the sofa behind us. "So…why the pow-wow?"

Sands rubbed his temples. "Seems as though we have a bit of a situation."

"Yeah. I figured. Last night's mess in the Flats. Am I right?" Sanchez asked wearily. "So, what's the play?"

"Well, first of all, we need to keep this under wraps until

the investigation is down the road a bit and we have at least half a clue of what's going on."

"The big cheeses?" Jake asked with a smirk.

"Some of us still have careers to think about," Sands answered curtly.

Jake nodded and looked away.

"So, no talking to the press, right?" I asked, looking directly at Jake and thinking specifically about his reporter pal, Jamal.

"Right. And for now, Maddie, you go down the alley and get up to speed on Jake's case."

"Great," I muttered under my breath.

Jake just smiled.

"But Lieu," Sanchez said, "the perp we like in the armed robbery case has a court date this afternoon—if he shows."

"Okay. Tomorrow, then. First thing."

Now I know how it feels for death row to get a call from the governor.

Lt. Sands stood up. So did the rest of us.

"So…tomorrow, then," Jake whispered touching my elbow. "I'm looking forward to it."

"Say hi to EC for me."

I was the first one out the door.

~~~

Protective Services

The social worker was parked at my desk when I came out of Lt. Sands' office. She looked like she wanted to be there about as much as I wanted to go down to Exit Alley. She was digging through her stuff in a disheveled search for something or other, first in her purse, then the briefcase, then in a huge Naugahyde bag stuffed with papers spilling out of manila file folders. I swear, most of them are one cat away from being a shopping cart lady. As I stepped over to my desk, she pulled her phone out of her coat pocket with a look of surprise, as if she had just accidentally performed a magic trick.

"You wanted to see me, detective?" the woman asked flatly without looking away from the screen. "It's been a long night."

"Yeah, well, welcome to our world. Murder doesn't always keep regular office hours."

"Murder?" She finally looked up at me.

I shook my head and went to get more coffee. Her eyes followed the steam rising from my mug like an oracle as I sat down at my desk. I didn't offer her any. I took a sip. "Yup. Murder."

"I didn't know."

"Huh," I said casually without putting on my shocked face. My inside voice said, *Imagine that—a clueless civil servant.* "How is Amy handling it?"

"Who?"

"Amy. The young woman you came for last night."

"Is she a suspect?"

I sighed. "If she was, she'd be here. She's a witness."

"Really?"

"Yes. *Really*. So, we need to make sure we keep tabs on her."

"We will find a good home for her." Her voice took on a snarky, *don't-tell-us-our-job* tone.

"What was wrong with the last six? I pulled up her sheet."

"Do you know how many files I have in my caseload?"

"Do you realize a child was found at a murder scene at three AM?"

"I don't have to sit here and take this."

"No, but you will if something happens to Amy."

The social worker stood and gathered up her worldly belongings. "I don't know what you mean."

"Yeah. You do."

She turned in a huff and shuffled out. I imagined her pushing a grocery cart with a shimmying wheel.

Sanchez

Sanchez took the social worker's place in the chair by my desk. She looked around the squad room, overtly nonchalant, then met and held my eye. "So…you want to fill me in?"

"Seems like there's an ugly wrinkle in my last case," I sighed. "Jake tried to warn me, but I ignored him. Everybody did."

"Ah, *El Toro.*" Sanchez patted the top of my hand. "If we didn't need the calves, they'd all be steers in my book."

I hung my head and chuckled to myself. She really had no use at all for men.

"And if he's not careful, he'll find himself between a couple of sesame seed buns."

"Well, I got a stay of execution for a day before I have to go down the alley to Artificial Crimes. Should we get something productive done?"

"Sure."

Sanchez came to the force by way of the municipal court where she was a bailiff, so she was plugged into the inner workings of the halls of justice. The perp I liked in one of my moldier cases, one she inherited when she was assigned to be my partner, had proved to be particularly slippery. Sanchez found his name on the docket for traffic court today, so we had planned on heading down to Part B to see if he showed up for his court date. If so, it'd be an easy collar.

From the time we hit the metal detectors at the entrance of the Justice Center until we got upstairs to traffic court, it was old home week for Sanchez. I learned more about kids, moms, and lovers than I ever could have imagined as she ran a gauntlet of gossip, providing a running narrative to me between the spurts of dialog. By the time we made it through I knew more about the workers in the Justice Center than I did about myself. At least I got a new recipe for mole sauce. We slipped into the courtroom as the clerk started calling out names to line up the defendants down the center aisle for their turn in the meat grinder of justice.

I sat down on the back bench as Sanchez went up to see if our perp's name had been called. As a deformed Catholic, I immediately began to squirm. The gallery benches were too much like pews. The front was like the chancel with blue-uniformed acolytes. And, of course, the judge's robes—not to mention the law's propensity for Latin—brought back too many Sunday morning memories of boredom at the hands of the Pope's minions. I guess I have PCSD: Post Church Stress Disorder. For a long, long time, I couldn't eat fish either. Still can't handle fish sticks.

Sanchez shook her head as she walked down the side aisle and slid in beside me. She whispered, "So, now we wait."

We witnessed the full menagerie of moving violations committed in our city as each defendant got to the head of the queue to take their turn in front of the judge, who dispensed justice in seven to ten-minute spurts, assessing fines, levying court costs, and assigning trial dates, depending on the severity of the infraction and whether an accident was involved. If only our cases could be tried so expeditiously, but felony murder tends to make for more lengthy and messy proceedings. Testifying was never one of my favorite duties.

Sanchez watched the proceedings like a mama grizzly fishing for salmon in a river. I had my doubts when we got partnered up after Walker decided to cash in his chips and retire on a high note once we rid the city of a serial killer. Can't blame him. At this point, with Jeffery's mutilated body in the Flats, I almost wished I had my twenty in to collect a pension, too. Despite her meter maid physique, Sanchez was a good cop. Nothing got by her. And though we were close to the same age, she was protective of me like a mama bear. We watched the proceedings in respectful silence, both passing our own judgments on the crowd even though we weren't wearing robes.

A long pause before the next case was called drew our eyes forward. The judge listened to a bailiff whisper in her ear and kept a careful sideways glare on the next defendant in line. Another bailiff sauntered down the center aisle with a stack of legal-sized manila folders calling out names to keep the queue loaded. She passed the end of the line and gave Sanchez a nod. I got up and slowly walked down the center. Sanchez slid to the outside and crept forward.

I worked my way up the line, shuffling defendants back until I was right behind our perp, who was growing impatient with the on-going discussion at the judge's bench. I glanced to see Sanchez flanking us to the left at the side of the room, then sidled up alongside him and leaned lightly against him.

My stalking must have worked because he instinctively jerked back and stiffened his spine. The angry look he shot my way melted when I gave him a coy, flirty smile. Downshifting into a cool, gangster slouch, he leered back up into my eyes and, nodding his head slightly as if approving of my looks, cracked a sneering half-smile exposing some custom gold grill work. I could only imagine there might be a woman somewhere who would find it alluring.

"Marcus Williams," the clerk called out.

It was our guy.

He glanced forward to notice two large male bailiffs coming towards him. When he turned back to me, I slid open my jacket to expose my badge and pulled the arrest warrant out of my breast pocket. The confusion on his face morphed into malice. The bailiffs were still ten feet away, but before he could raise his arms to lay hands on me, Sanchez had her vice-grip on his elbow and his left wrist already in cuffs.

I grabbed his right arm as he turned to resist. "Don't. Don't do it. Walk out like a man or all us girls will giggle at you when those guys drag your ass out of here."

"You bitch."

I twisted his arm back for Sanchez to cuff it. "You don't know the half of it."

"Come on, *Ferdinand,*" Sanchez teased. "Let's get you into your pen."

Each bailiff took an arm and hustled Williams out of the front of the courtroom.

"Thanks," I said to Sanchez. "That was easy."

"No sense in breaking a sweat," she answered. "One last good one before you go into exile, huh?"

As we followed our collar out, the clerk called the next case. "Victor Stanislov — Disobedience to a stop sign; speeding sixty-three in a thirty-five mile an hour zone; failure to wear a seatbelt. How do you plead?"

The Darknet

Sounds like Jake, I thought to myself.
"No contest, your honor," I heard behind me as we left.

Exit Alley

I woke up bug-eyed at four-thirty in the morning and stared at my bedroom ceiling for at least an hour. Going "down the alley" was definitely the wrong direction for any career in law enforcement to be headed. On top of that, I would be paired up with Jake again. How could such a great thing have gone so sideways? Sure, he saved my life, but…Munchausen bait?

And the business with Jamal. I should have listened to Jake, but it was the mother of all cases. And it was mine. I'm guessing the gratitude of the city will be fleeting when the truth is known.

Then, of course, there was waitress Amy. Jake certainly didn't take his time about it.

When I hit that wall, I got up and dressed for a run. There'd be no shoppers that early, so I could run the streets, then hit the greenbelt to the Metropark. I didn't have to look at my watch to know I was taking longer than I should, passing my usual two-and-a-half-mile turn around mark. I just kept going deeper into the woods, mesmerized by the slap of sole against asphalt until my mind finally cleared of the troublesome thoughts that woke me.

Back again at Crocker Park, customers were just starting to gather at Starbucks like lint in the dryer trap. I got a *Venti* dark roast and blew that pop stand quick before the temptation of the pastry counter won out.

I purposely took my sweet time over a container of yogurt, reading deeper than usual into the morning news stories and stopping uncharacteristically to listen to entire segments on the *Today* show that usually passed for background noise. Thoughts of Jake were countered at the bathroom mirror by contemplating whether I should cut my hair. Then, of course, *What should I wear?* became a debate worthy of even Socrates, Aristotle, and Sartre. *Sartre?* And there was Jake invading my thoughts again through the back door.

Being in no hurry for my new assignment with the Geek Squad—even if it was only temporary—*and it would be temporary*—I by-passed I90 and took the scenic route to work down Lake Road knowing I'd be fashionably late.

And late I was. When the mousy little nerd showed me into the darkened conference room in Exit Alley, the briefing was already underway. No one—not even Jake—said anything, so I took a seat in the back of the room and surveyed the audience. Besides Jake and his partner, EC, there were a half dozen obvious keyboard jockeys in attendance, along with a bored Mutt-and-Jeff pair dressed in coveralls parked at the back of the room with me. At least Lt. Sands wasn't there to see I was late. I actually wished I was back in the House doing paperwork with Sanchez on yesterday's collar. Everyone but Jake followed along on their *iSlates*. He stared at the presentation slide projected behind the guy he called "Q"—at least I assumed it was Q from his descriptions of the head-hacker-what's-in-charge. The slide showed a map of the metropolitan area splattered with red dots, which were the locations of unsolved murders. I wondered if the victims in my last case were up there, too, but downtown and the Flats were covered by one big indistinct puddle of red.

The Darknet

As Q gave an eye-glazing recitation of the city's crime statistics, I wondered why every unsolved homicide had suddenly become our concern.

"You can gray out all the cases prior to 2030," EC instructed Q. "That's when the FTA approved and released synthoid PSAs for licensing and commercial deployment."

"Yeah, well, you know, there were government-approved trial runs going on before that," said the shorter, rounder, and balder of my coverall companions in the back row.

Huh. I would not have guessed they were actually paying attention.

"Twenty twenty-three," barked his companion, Puff, which I knew from the script in the embroidered oval over his heart.

"Could have been. Yup. Maybe," answered his partner as he adjusted his wire-rimmed glasses. "But the early trials were restricted to academic and industrial campuses, mostly in Silicon Valley and Boston."

"Q, can you do a split screen with EC's filter on the right, using what, 2025?" Jake turned and asked EC beside him.

"That's good," EC answered.

"And on the left put up twentieth century-only cold cases along with suspected serials and sprees from, ah, just put 1850 in for drill, and let's see what we get."

"Eighteen fifty? Seriously?" one of the nerds asked in a smarmy tone. "I don't get what these data points will demonstrate."

I didn't either, but I found there were a lot of times that Jake's way of thinking was like taking the scenic route—certainly not the most direct path, but you go with it because it always took you someplace interesting.

Q gave the gangly questioner the hairy eyeball, then went ahead and split the screen. Dots faded, and new ones bloomed as the filters were applied.

"Well, well, well…Looky there." Jake smiled at the Digital Doubting Thomas. "A *ruby* necklace."

Even Q was clearly confused by what Jake meant. I wasn't. A long strand of parks ringed the metropolitan area from Huntington Beach in the western suburbs south to the turnpike, then around north again to the lake at the easternmost edge of the county. It was called the "Emerald Necklace" from how the Metroparks system looks on a map of the city. I was guessing the pale, nerdy kids in Exit Alley didn't get out of doors much. Red dots on both halves of the screen formed a blood trail through the park system.

"Q, pull all these case files and have your team start looking for links," Jake said standing up and walking to the front of the conference room. He pointed to a red dot in Bay Village on the new side of the screen. I noticed it was mirrored on the map of historical cases. "Get me this one right away."

"Why's that?" Q asked.

"Maddie and I are going to take a ride."

Like I said, *the scenic route.*

The Crime of the Century

"You've got your slab, right?" Jake asked as we headed towards the parking lot. "I forgot mine."

"Of course," I sighed shaking my head. Typical Jake move. His techno-fossil attitude must really drive the digital tribe down the alley insane. I'm surprised one of them hasn't tried to bash his head in with a keyboard. Of course, that'd be the fast track to becoming a binary zero. "You want me to drive?"

"Nah. I got this." Jake veered away from the squad cars towards the employee lot.

A warm dread spilled down through my chest as I caught sight of Jake's car. *That bastard.* He knew. Of course he did.

I was an automotive agnostic before Jake—just a tool to get me from here to there—and as perplexed as the rest of my half of the species as to the passions that welled up out of testosterone for fossil-fueled vehicles. But Jake had restored a convertible-top car from the last century that he was kind of prissy about. If I was still going to church, I'd have to include in confession that I really enjoyed our Sunday afternoon drives through the park, down the lakeshore or busting every speed limit on the winding back roads of Amish country. It was fun just going, not having a destination in mind but always finding one.

I split off from Jake and rounded the trunk to the

passenger side. "Jesus. Where do you even find gasoline for this thing?"

"Race tracks, marinas, and airports mainly."

"Shouldn't we call Bay Village PD and let them know we're coming?"

"Nah, it's just a day at the beach for a dashing young couple," Jake answered over the ragtop of his shiny black *Mustang*.

"A dashing young couple carrying badges and packing heat."

"Packing heat?" Jake tossed a lecherous smile my way.

"Glocks, you moron."

"Yeah…right…"

We got in, and Jake put the top down. He pulled out of the lot, zipped down to Lakeside, then merged onto the Main Avenue Bridge over the Flats where the river spilled into the lake. The highway would have been faster, but I enjoyed the ride along the shoreline. And Jake let me enjoy it by not trying to make small talk. He knew, *that bastard.*

When we got to the westernmost link in the Metroparks "Emerald Necklace," Jake passed by the entrance. I had learned not to point out the obvious with him and said nothing. Just past the park, he slowed to eyeball the houses built on the lake. After trolling past four or five of them, he sped up, then turned around in a church parking lot.

"So, whatcha looking for?"

"The crime of the century—well, last century…one of them anyway," Jake said looking back over his shoulder. He squealed the tires pulling out of the lot.

"And which crime of the century is that?"

He took his eyes off the road to stare my way. I could read

his eyes even behind the sunglasses and knew what he was going to say: "Those who cannot remember the past—"

"Yeah, yeah yeah—are condemned to repeat it. You've told me that a million times."

"...*condemned to repeat it.*" Jake muttered it more to himself than to me.

"What is it?"

Jake pulled the *Mustang* into Huntington Beach and parked. "Let's take a walk on the beach and when we're done, maybe I'll buy you an ice cream cone. Don't forget your slab."

I grabbed my *iSlate*. Parallel concrete stairways led down the fifty-foot cliff to the beach. We stopped on the landing halfway down that formed a long sight seeing balcony. Jake leaned on the rail and looked east towards downtown. I braced myself for "the talk" we probably should have had when we broke up but never did.

"Down there. By the big tree." Jake pointed to a huge, solitary oak tree growing at the water's edge. "That's where they found her, right?"

"Huh? What?" My mind scrambled to get back into cop mode.

"Q sent you the case file, didn't he?"

"Let me look." I quickly lit up my *iSlate* and swiped until I found it.

"Brunette. Shoulder-length hair," Jake recited. "About thirty-one or so. Bludgeoned to death. Found in a nightgown with her legs dangling into the water."

I scanned the police report. There was a picture of the body that matched his description. "Yeah. So, you've already read the case file?"

"Nope." Jake shook his head. "No murder weapon?"

"Doesn't look like one was found."

"Check the autopsy report. Pregnant?"

I swiped through the murder book. Right again. "What are we doing here? Parlor tricks? You're clairvoyant now?"

Jake stood up from the rail. He paused to give me a serious look, then scaled down the rest of the steps to the beach. I followed him out to the tree, but stood back behind him ten feet or so to give him some space as he stared at the concrete block pier where the murder took place. It was part of his process to tune himself into the crime scene. We all do it different. Jake taught me that—and that you don't mess with another person's style. It wasn't *déjà vu,* but it felt damn familiar. And it should have after all the cases we worked. He'd come out of his meditation soon enough, so I watched the waves roll off the lake onto the beach. The water was deep blue. The sun was warm, but the wind had a bite of chill in it.

"A Munchausen." Jake finally said into the wind.

"Huh? You talking to me or yourself?"

Jake looked back at me.

"A robot? But Jake, her head was bashed in pretty badly. That's a crime of passion."

"It might have been. A hundred years ago. It's what I've thought all along though…and feared."

"But you haven't even read the case."

"Didn't have to really. I read the other one."

"What other one?"

"The crime of the century. For Cleveland anyway."

"What are you talking about?"

Jake started walking west. I fell in beside him, and we

pushed slowly through the loose sand. "Nineteen fifty-four. The Sam Sheppard case. His pregnant wife, Marilyn, was bludgeoned to death. There." Jake pointed to the houses up on the bluff we had trolled by earlier. "The house is long gone. But this is where it happened."

"But, that's ancient history."

"Yup. But those who cannot remember—"

"—the past are condemned to repeat it…Copycat crimes?"

"More like digital replications."

"By synthoids? How many more?"

"Your last, for one."

"The hookers in the Flats?"

"Jack the Ripper."

I felt my shoulders slump. I should have listened to him. "I don't like this. I don't like this at all."

"No one will." Jake put his arm around my waist and pulled me to head back towards the stairs up the bluff. "How about that ice cream cone, little girl?"

In the Wind

Sanchez bolted up from her desk and met me at the door to the squad room. "She's in the wind."

"Huh? Who's in the wind?"

"Amy."

"Amy? Why the hell should I care—" Then I noticed the CPS social worker making a hasty exit out the back. *Oh, that Amy.* "You! Cat Lady. Hold it—"

Sanchez sidestepped in front of me, blocking my path. "Cool it, *la roja*. Let her go. I got all the info and talked to the sarge about stepping up patrols under the bridges."

I stood and fumed.

"So, what's with the new look? You set your hair dryer on turbo?"

I tuned back into the moment and smiled wearily at Sanchez. "Jake's convertible."

"Those things aren't really safe, you know. Especially not if he's behind the wheel." Then she read something in the look on my face. "What's wrong?"

"Amy. She saw what happened. They'll come for her."

"Yeah, well, it's not like the kid shops at Amazon or anything, so without digital footprints, they can't cybertrack her either. We'll have the advantage with the number of eyeballs actually out on the street looking for the kid."

"We've got to find her before they do."

"And who's they? Do the Brainiacs down the alley have any clue?"

I shook my head.

"And what were you and Jake doing all morning? Joyriding in his rat rod?"

"Have you had lunch?"

"Nope. You buying?"

"Better yet. We'll make Jake pay."

"Then I'm in. I am definitely in."

I fixed my hair, and we walked over to Cutty's Delicatessen. Jake and EC were sitting on opposite sides of a booth in the back.

"What is this? Some kind of half-assed double date?" Sanchez threw a stern look back and forth between Jake and EC, then, thankfully, slid in beside Jake. "And you keep your hands to yourself, Mr. Jake."

"Hi, EC," I said smiling his way. I sat down catty-corner from Jake. "How've you been?"

"Good, Maddie. Nice to see you again."

I nudged EC with my elbow and leaned in to whisper, "Maybe we can shake these losers and take in a film or something."

EC smiled.

"Hey, hey, hey—everybody, hands on the table," Jake scolded. "No monkey business."

I blew gently into EC's ear with a sideways glance at Jake.

EC blushed.

Jake smirked back.

"Seriously? It's like a high school lunchroom in here."

Sanchez scowled. "Hand me a damn menu. What's good here?"

"Well, hey there, missy Madeline," Cutty said ambling up to the table, emphasizing the "line" in my name. "It's been a while. How's your Pop?"

"Hi, Officer Cutler," I gushed feigning childhood innocence. He leered at me like he always did, like an uncle you never wanted to get too close to at holiday family get-togethers. He had been my Dad's partner for a while. Jake's, too, when he just got out of the academy. "He's doing well. Thank you."

Cutty took a long, loud slurp of scotch out of the department mug "liberated" from the House when he retired. He cocked his head at Jake and then back at me. "Hmmm."

I just smiled. "I'll have the usual."

"A salad? Aw, you're killing me, Madeline."

"Pastrami Reuben," Jake piped in.

"Ditto," said EC.

Cutty stared down at Sanchez as she studied the menu like a crime scene photo. *"Detective…"*

"The chicken salad. Fresh?"

"Of course."

"Fresh today?"

"Well…"

"Uh-huh. I thought so."

"Sheesh. Tough customer." Cutty looked at me, then Jake.

"You better just bring me that meatloaf—and make sure there's extra gravy on it." Sanchez snapped her menu shut and handed it to Cutty. "In case it's too dry."

"Yes, ma'am. Right away, ma'am."

"That's more like it. And bring me a Pepsi-Cola."

Cutty shook his head as he retreated with his marching orders.

"So, what did Q come up with?" Jake asked EC. "What dots did they connect between the cases?"

"Nothing yet. They were still involved in an animated debate over programming algorithms when I gave up and started pulling files manually. There's a lot, Jake. A lot."

"What the what." Jake looked at Sanchez. "See what I have to put up with?"

"You made that bed you're lyin' in, mister." Of course, Sanchez knew the score on Jake and me. "I never shot no councilman's son. Maddie neither."

Well, maybe she didn't really know *everything*.

"Means, motive, victim, scene, time of day." Jake counted them off on his fingers. "It's simple, but no. They've always got to reinvent what Gates and Jobs figured out nearly a hundred years ago."

"Who?"

Jake slapped his hand over his eyes and shook his head wearily.

"Sounds like a kid's game: Gates and Jobs…Jobs and Gates." Sanchez poked her thumb in Jake's direction, then asked me, "You and…*him?*"

I just shrugged my shoulders.

With no police business to discuss, the lunch degenerated into a session of good-natured juvenile banter and teasing until EC got a call. Sanchez and I watched seriousness melt the merriment off his face as he listened. Jake finished his Reuben.

"That was Q. There's been a fresh one," EC explained with a heavy sigh. "In District Four."

"Let me guess." Jake licked the Thousand Island salad dressing off his fingers, then wiped them clean with his napkin. "No head. And the balls were cut off."

EC slowly started to nod.

"What the—how'd you—" Sanchez stuttered.

"Voodoo." Jake gave Sanchez a long sideways stare.

"I'm Hispanic, not Haitian."

"Whatever."

"He thinks he's psychic now," I explained. "Right?"

Jake shrugged. "So, ladies, would you care to join us for a sunny afternoon jaunt to a crime scene?"

As we left, Jake told Cutty to put lunch on his tab.

Kingsbury Run

We got there about the same time as the CSI van. There is a certain reverence about a murder scene. It's busy, sure, but busy like communion at church. Lots of purposeful, muted movements. Hushed conversations. Footsteps like Iroquois stalking through the woods in moccasins. A death at center stage. Sanchez actually crossed herself as we paused at the crime scene tape, which wrapped off an urban wooded area just south of the Red Line Rapid Transit tracks off Grand Avenue.

"Whatcha got?" Jake asked a detective who approached us on the opposite side of the tape.

"Murder most foul," he answered and extended his hand. "Wally."

"So I heard. Jake." They shook hands, and Jake made a quick round of introductions. "Mind if I—we take a look." He threw a thumb in my direction.

Wally shrugged and held up the yellow tape for us to duck under. He motioned EC and Sanchez to follow, too. "Not really going to disturb anything. The vic's been here long enough for the coyotes to find him. So, what's Artificial Crimes doing out here? Kind of off your regular beat, isn't it?"

"Looking for patterns."

"You got another dead headless horseman out there?"

"Not really. The location threw up a red flag from our tech guys."

Wally shook his head. "How many flags you guys got? It's a dumping grounds along here."

"Has been for a long time."

Wally stopped about ten feet from the body. He sighed heavily and scratched the back of his neck. Discolored with bloated limbs, the headless torso had been ripped open and hollowed out by hungry scavengers.

"Hey, thanks. Good luck," Jake said and abruptly turned to head back to the car.

Wally gave us a quizzical look.

"That's it?" Sanchez asked me.

EC and I smiled. I reached out to shake the detective's hand. "Thanks, Wally. Looks like the forensics team is ready to go. We'll get out of your way."

"What is it with him?" Sanchez asked as we trailed behind Jake.

"He saw what he needed to see," EC explained. "No need to hang around and make a career out of it."

"And what did he see?"

"I'm sure we'll get a lecture on it in due time."

I just smiled.

Jake was leaning against the car scanning the area up and down the tracks.

"So, Sherlock, what have you got?" EC teased.

"They used to call it Kingsbury Run after the dude who settled here eons ago. Became a shanty town in the depression before World War II last century. Starts by the river up in the Flats and basically follows the tracks out to Shaker."

"Yeah…so?" Sanchez asked impatiently.

Jake looked up the tracks towards downtown. "It's where the Torso Murderer's victims ended up. A serial killer who cut off the victim's heads. The men usually lost their other brain, too."

EC's chuckle drew a scowl from Sanchez. She looked back at Jake. "Like I said, yeah…so?"

"You should check out the CPD museum sometime."

Sanchez shot me a "what the hell" expression. I nodded. "Been there. Done that. Got the t-shirt."

"Thirteen documented. But, really, probably thirty or more—at least around here. They say the killer was also active in Pittsburgh. And they even tried to pin a murder in LA on him. The Black Dahlia. Never caught the perp. It killed the career of the original *Untouchable*."

"Elliot Ness," EC explained.

I'm sure EC's been to the museum, too. A few times.

Jake nodded and smiled.

"You solving crimes hundreds of years old?" Sanchez asked incredulously. "I figure we got our hands full in the here and now, don't you?"

Sanchez looked my way. I shrugged.

"That body wasn't a hundred years old." Jake pointed to where Wally stood watching the Bunny Suit Boys process his crime scene. Jake looked skyward. "In fact, I'm surprised we don't have buzzards overhead."

"Yup. And that's District Four's headache."

Jake smiled down at Sanchez. "Yeah. You'd think."

~~

The Muni Lot

As I came down the alley to Artificial Crimes the next morning, Q was outside slouched against the wall with a pouty look on his face, swiping furiously at his *iSlate*. "Shouldn't you be inside getting ready for the briefing?"

Q grunted. "A little change in agenda. Some synthoid's run amuck down in the Muni Lot. Smashing windshields, I guess. Jake and EC caught the call and went to bring it to heel."

I shuddered. The Muni Lot parking garage at the west end was where Jake shot the councilman's son. "How long ago?"

"Just left a few minutes ago. You can probably still catch the show." Q never looked up from his *iSlate,* so I doubt he even noticed I had already started off in that direction.

It was maybe a ten-minute walk and a fifteen-minute drive by the time I checked out a car and waited on traffic lights, so I decided to head down there on foot. About halfway, the adrenalin pumping through my veins reached my feet, and I found myself jogging down Lakeside towards East Ninth. It was a good thing I didn't have Sanchez in tow.

When I turned the corner towards the lake, the East Ninth garage entrance was cordoned off. Jake and EC were at the tac van suiting up to go in. I flashed my badge to patrol and crossed over.

"What's going on?" I asked breathlessly. I guess I had been

running harder than I thought.

Jake shot me a look like he caught the nervousness in my voice.

"Q said you were down here."

"One of the city sweepers went off the rails, grabbed a hammer, and started smashing headlights and windshields down by the Rock Hall. Then it ducked into the garage," EC explained. "They're old units, and the city stopped ponying up for the OS updates a while back, so they get cranky sometimes. This shouldn't take long."

"Yeah. We'll get in, get out…" Jake said, strapping up his vest.

EC finished Jake's thought with a chuckle. "And nobody'll get hurt…*we hope.*"

"A walk in the park." Jake winked at me, then put on his *Google Glass* and his helmet.

A dark memory sucked the breath out of my lungs. It was the same thing he said after he swapped out his magazine and put mine—with one less cartridge in it—into his Glock, then followed the wounded councilman's son into the parking garage.

The piercing squeal of Jake's *eM&P* pistol as it armed and charged made me grimace. I hated that sound ever since the alley in the Flats. It was the one thing I actually remembered from the synthoid attack on me and, even though it saved my life, it brought back a very bad moment. Now there were two bad memories floating in my head as I watched Jake and EC get swallowed up by the mouth of the garage.

I went over to the Command Vehicle and rapped on the side.

"Hey, Maddie. Come on in." Sergeant Kovacic, the SWAT

team leader, motioned me into the back of the step van. "Welcome to the show."

I stood behind him and scanned the bank of monitors. On the right was the feed from Jake's *Google Glass*. EC was on the left. Center stage was the tap into the garage security system and up top was the feed from the ePD scanning app on EC's *iSlate*. Kovacic scouted ahead of them, paging and panning through the camera feeds floor-by-floor to locate the city's wayward synthoid. Along the inside row of cars, tailgate and rear windows were pocked with what looked like giant bullet holes from where they were struck with the hammer.

I looked over my shoulder outside the van and saw that SWAT had taken up positions at the garage entrance, just in case.

"No joy," EC said over the comm channel. "Moving to level two."

"Sweep is clear to two so far," Kovacic answered. "Watch the blind spots at the ends."

I found my eyes drawn to Jake's visual feed and couldn't help but let my thoughts be pulled back to that night when Sara Ann's murder case went sideways and shuffled Jake out of Robbery/Homicide and down the alley to chase robots. I was green and got too anxious and careless and let myself get jumped. I guess the councilman's son didn't realize he was being tailed by detectives who suspected him of murder when he ducked into the parking garage at two AM and ambushed me with other ideas in mind. Jake saw and bolted across East Ninth Street, but my instincts just kicked in. Since the perps's hands were full grabbing my private parts, I was able to get my weapon out and fired a round into his leg. He dazed me by throwing me hard into the back end of a sedan, drew on me, but saw Jake coming at him and bolted up the ramp. As I shook the cobwebs from my head, four more shots echoed down from above—one smaller caliber and three from Jake's Glock. It wasn't until the shooting team checked my weapon that I realized that my gun was fully loaded. Jake gave me a look and took the whole shooting on himself. Politics being what it is, he got demoted to the Artificial Crimes Unit. Work partners no more, during his suspension, we became…well, *involved.*

Jake's view through the monitor panned methodically left, then right. Then left again. They turned the corner, and Jake's eyes paused on the big "Level 3" painted on a pillar. That's where he shot the councilman's son. He turned his head back over his shoulder like he was looking directly at me through the monitor, then moved on, eyes forward again. Up ahead, silhouetted against the outside light at the end of the aisle, was a human-like figure holding a raised hammer. I shuddered at the sight.

"Halt! Police!" EC's command echoed back thinly through the comm channel.

Kovacic quickly paged back and forth through the security camera feeds until he found the best angle and zoomed it to take in the scene over Jake's and EC's shoulders.

The synthoid froze, hammer poised above its head. Jake's monitor was filled with his sight view down the barrel of his *eM&P.*

I could see from the ePD scanning app screen remoted into the monitor bank that EC was trying to establish a channel link to the synthoid's operating system.

The Darknet

Jake's *Glass* status flashed green. He had a confirmed frequency lock on the droid with his EMP pistol.

The synthoid remained frozen like a statue. Kovacic zoomed in on it.

I could only imagine in the static, flat screen images before me that electrons and digital signals were flying furiously through the air between EC, Jake, and the AnSub.

"What the hell?" EC looked up from his *iSlate* screen at the synthoid as it let the hammer drop from its hand, fell to its knees, and put its hands behind its head.

It was too far away for the words to be audible, but the simultaneous text message that appeared on the ePD app screen, as well as the *Google Glass* feeds was clear: "I SURRENDER, JAKE."

~~~

Would You Know My Name

We sat around the conference table on Q's side of Exit Alley waiting for Jake: EC, Q and me. Q's *iSlate* lay flat and dark on the table in front of him. I can't ever recall him being so…unfidgety. It was eerie. He just stared off into space.

EC doodled aimlessly on a yellow legal pad.

I couldn't fathom why everyone was so moody. The takedown of the synthoid in the parking garage seemed to me to have gone off without a hitch or even much drama, but obviously, something happened that I missed to put everyone in a funk. Jake had gone down to the Captain's office to explain the facts of life to the civil servant from the Division of Streets about why they weren't going to get their robot garbage picker-upper back. So, we waited, and I caught up on my real case load with Sanchez.

Marcus Williams didn't make bail, and a prelim was scheduled for the eighteenth. It was an open-and-shut case, but when you've got a public defender and the bill for legal fees doesn't come to your house, you milk the system and get your money's worth—I mean the taxpayer's money's worth. Still no sighting of Amy by patrol yet. I sighed loud enough that Q and EC both looked my way.

Just then, Jake appeared at the door to the conference room and rolled his eyes up into the back of his head. He tossed his *iNode* into the middle of the table and motioned toward the exit with his head. The boys anted up their electronics into the pot and slid out past Jake.

"Come on, Mads. You in or out?" He looked down the hall towards the exit. "Eyes and ears only."

I unclipped my *iNode* and slid it forward.

"Phone, too."

"Sounds serious," I said, pushing my phone forward.

"Eh…"

Jake chivalrously stepped back to let me out the door. Down at the end of the hall, Q tapped away at what I presumed was a burner phone. When we went outside, they all looked up at the security camera above the door to make sure the power light was off. Nobody said anything.

"What?" I finally asked impatiently.

"My name," Jake mumbled. "It said my name."

I still didn't get it.

"I surrender…*Jake.*"

"So?"

"It's personal," explained EC. "Like people, droids don't get personal with strangers they've never met. How could it know Jake's name?"

"Maybe it read it off the chip in your badge," I offered. "You know, like when we swipe it to log in."

Q shook his head. "That info is pretty deeply encrypted in the system. For tactical reasons. Too risky to broadcast in the clear to John Q."

"Facial recognition?"

EC exhaled loudly through his pursed lips and shook his head slowly. "RSHA…and, of course, the ACLU."

"Huh?"

"Robotic Safety and Health Administration," Q said clearing his throat.

"I know what RSHA stands for."

"Fourth Amendment, right to privacy, yada yada yada," Jake said dismissively. "Damn lawyers."

Q saw from the look on my face that I didn't get it. "Early on, there were a bunch of lawsuits, so the Justice Department and the industry came up with a consent decree for intelligence gathering on citizens by socially embedded entities. While they can passively record, synthoids can't actively catalog individualized metadata on citizens."

"What's that mean?"

"It means that while synthoids certainly have facial recognition capabilities, legally their software must be structured to be task specific with limited access only to appropriate database libraries. A security guard synthoid would be programmed to do facial matching against the database of a company or agency employee roster, just like a human guard would know the people who came in and out of the building every day. A low-level municipal street sweeper would probably have Department of Streets employees resident in its memory banks and maybe access to the U.S. Marshal's fugitive database, but not much more. Not even law enforcement units have unrestricted access to AFFRIS."

"So, for this thing to call Jake by name…"

"Means that someone hacked it and planted my name there."

"Munchausen? The Baron?"

Q shrugged his shoulders. "We'll have to see what we get out of the synthoid when Mechanical is done."

"I guess this time it's personal." Jake opened up the door to Exit Alley. "Come on, let's get our electronic leashes and go see Bob and Puff."

Bob and Puff

"Puff?" I asked Jake. "As in Puff the Magic Dragon?"

He stopped in the middle of the hallway on our way to Mechanical and stared at me with a bemused smirk growing on his face.

"What?"

Jake shook his head. "Wow. That's a cultural reference out of the antiquities."

"And you say I never pay attention when you talk."

"Well, then, I stand corrected," Jake chuckled. "As for the origins of his name, ah, let's just say that Mr. Puff is not really the sharing type. Nobody knows. Not even Bob."

"Great. Yet another victim of testosterone poisoning."

"We're all damaged goods in our own way." Jake shrugged and continued on down the hall.

I picked up my pace to catch up with him. "Is that a confession or just more bragging?"

Jake stopped at the door labeled "Technical Forensic Lab" and paused. "Look, just don't ask any dumb questions."

"Hey—"

"Puff does not suffer fools lightly and, as entertaining as it is sometimes, I'm not in the mood for one of his lectures."

We pushed into the Lab. I hadn't been there before, and it was kind of creepy just like Jake described it to me in the past:

a strange mix of a robot morgue—the street cleaning synthoid was laid out on a table with its guts exposed—but also an electronics junkyard lined with shelves crammed with circuit boards, wires, motorized actuators, and who knows what else in overflowing Tupperware bins. Heads and various other body parts hung from the ceiling off to the sides of the room. There was a vague whiff of machine shop oil in the air. A Mutt-and-Jeff pair from central casting stood over the synthoid, and I immediately recognized the shorter, chunkier, and friendlier bespectacled Bob and his cohort, the tall, lean-and-mean nearsighted Puff.

"Hey, Jakie." Bob looked up from the abdomen of the synthoid and beamed a huge smile. He pushed his way around Puff to get to our side of the table. Wiping his hands on a soiled cloth and adjusting the wire-rimmed glasses on his face, Bob gave me a not too subtle once over with his eyes. "Wow. Traveling in style I see. A bit out of your league, wouldn't you say?"

"I'm Maddie," I said and extended my hand before Jake could make some wisecrack. We shook hands. His felt slick with oil even though he had just wiped it off.

"Hi, Maddie. Pleased to meet you." Bob held onto the handshake a bit too long. "You know Jake, here, used to talk about you a lot. Not so much anymore."

"Well, ah…" I could feel myself blushing, and Bob obviously saw it.

"Boy, I can't even imagine if one of these things went beserkoid on me in some dark alley in the middle of the night." Bob smiled and looked from me to Jake, then back to me. "That last case was, well, a doozie. Sorry it was such a close call for you. Anyway, it's his loss for sure." Bob pointed at Jake with his thumb.

Puff groaned loudly behind Bob. "Jesus, cheese and jam on a cracker already. Are we done with the tea and crumpets yet?"

"And good day to you, too, eh, Puff?" Jake said sweetly.

"Don't try to make Canadian nice-nice with me. I got no use for 'em or for you neither."

Jake looked at me. "I told you."

"Don't mind ol' Puff here," Bob chuckled. "He's more bark than bite."

Puff growled just loud enough to be heard and bared his teeth.

Bob stepped back in mock fear. "Down, boy. Down."

"Boys, boys, boys…let's not make a fuss over the lady," Jake said, wagging a finger at them. "I don't think any of us here are her type…anymore anyway."

I put my hand on Bob's shoulder and rubbed lightly. "Oh, I don't know. This one is kind of cute."

This time it was Bob's turn to blush.

"Tea and crumpets," Puff mumbled. "Can we help you with something? If not, get along then."

"Anything on the street sweeper?" Jake asked, meeting Puff's squinty-eyed stare.

"Should have been put out to pasture a long time ago," Bob said to Jake but looked at me and smiled. "Gen two. Early rev level. Haven't seen any evidence of it being chopped."

Bob read the quizzical look on my face.

"Unauthorized physical modifications," Bob explained to me with a big toothy grin. "Any repairs, parts replacements, or upgrades have to be logged and verified at the biennial inspection before recertification. Got a clean bill of health on the paperwork."

"Gen twos were solid machines," Puff said, looking down into the android's abdomen and poking around with his finger as if he had dropped a coin in it. "Nothing really fancy. But damned reliable. Vertically integrated manufacturing helped. There's still a lot of them out there. More than you'd think."

"Yeah. I can't see the city springing for the latest and greatest just to pick up litter in the Muni Lot," Jake said.

Puffed glanced sideways at Jake. "Gets the job done. What else do you need?"

"So, nothing mechanical?" I asked.

"Highly unlikely," said Bob. "I'd have Q take a close look at the security patches. It's been a problem keeping them current with so many and, oh, I don't know, maybe the Streets Department's IT guys haven't been diligent about updates—if you know what I mean."

"I do," Jake answered. "I do."

"We'll have the memory modules over to him to dump by tomorrow."

"Thanks, Bob."

"So, what are you hanging around bugging us for?" Puff straightened up and stared at Jake. "Leave already."

"Aw, Puff…Didn't we brighten your day even just a tad?"

For the first time, Puff looked at me. "Her, maybe. You? Not so much."

~~~

Phantom Evil

So, there was nothing to do but wait. No sense in doing it down in Exit Alley. I don't really belong. Normally, I would have at least stopped by my desk in Robbery/Homicide, but with my reassignment, I was even feeling a bit of a square peg in a round hole there as well. Plus, if Sanchez was still around—besides her personality taking a heavy toll in and of itself—she'd make me go through every moment of my exile with Jake. I didn't need a grilling.

I was tempted to take a leisurely ride home along the lake, but that was the way Jake took to the Sheppard crime scene and re-enactment at Huntington Beach. So, I allowed myself to be grid locked on the highway out of downtown. In the quiet corpuscle of my car, time stopped and passed simultaneously as I amoebaed my way home. No radio. No thoughts. Just floating along in the four-lane blood red flow of brake lights until the car parked itself.

Usually, the commute home serves to purge the workday and its worries from my mind, but as I walked along the sidewalk crowded with shoppers, diners, drinkers, and movie goers, I started searching for *them*. Jake explained it a hundred times—or so it seemed—and I never got it. But now I cared like I never did before—straining to see, trying to find a constellation in a field of stars. But if you don't know already, all you see are points of light. The images don't come and nothing in the sky makes sense like it does to others who know.

I got a bowl of lobster bisque to go from the deli around the corner, but it cooled on the counter as I poured a big glass of cab and stood at the window watching the foot traffic down below.

In all of my crime-fighting experience, evil was always incarnate in the man. Now evil, unmoored, floated free among us. And I could not see it.

In the morning, I dumped the cold bisque and went back to work.

Old News

I got to my desk early. Like just before six, well before the day tour officially started. I still can't really believe it, but in some ways, I was turning into my dad. He was always up hours before the rest of us. He'd be on his way out the door before me and my brothers dragged ourselves out of bed for school. I never really got it, until my day got crammed full of the demands of others, too. A half-hour or so alone at my desk with a cup of coffee centered me for the day and let me get one up on it. Unfortunately…

"Hey, Detective." Jake's reporter buddy, Jamal—aka E.J. Quick in print—was parked next to my desk, as out of place in the House as a rat rod in the Pepper Pike Country Club valet lot. "Top of the morning to you."

"We are not all Irish, you know." I cruised on by to the coffee machine, pulled down my *Wizard of Oz* cup and inspected the pot.

"I just made that about twenty minutes ago," Jamal called out, raising a department mug. "Elliot said to go ahead."

I shrugged and poured a cup. I took a sip and was momentarily thankful to at least start my day with a fresh brew rather than graveyard sludge. I walked back to my desk and sat down. "So, how are you here and why are you here?"

"Not stalking. Not stalking." Jamal raised his hands in mock surrender.

"Did Jake put you up to this?"

The reporter slowly shook his head. Jake trusted Jamal. I didn't. I didn't trust any of them. And when I found out the two of them were swapping inside information on my last case, I hit the roof, convinced that was what almost got me killed by the synthoid in that alley. Jake tried and tried to explain how it was a two-way street, but in my mind, he crossed a serious line. Terminally serious. That's me: stubborn, like my dad.

"No. Jake doesn't know I'm here."

"So, why?"

Jamal took a measured sip of his coffee. "Business."

"Of course. 'Cause we're not friends."

"Look, we both have our roles. We both have our *jobs* to do. We both have to scratch out a living and make it home at night. It doesn't mean we have to gouge each other's eyes out."

"What? Are you actually calling for a truce?"

"*Realpolitik*. We may not wear the same uniform, but that doesn't mean we're not on the same side. Jake gets it—"

"Don't. Don't even go there."

"No problem. I get it. Old news. Old wounds. But a pain that lingers is not always the next injury."

"What do you mean?"

"Do you want to end up in Exit Alley? Permanently like Jake?"

Inside, I could feel my chest tighten, reflexively answering Jamal's question.

"Your last case was a stink bomb. Not your fault, but, still, you got blue dye splattered on you."

"No thanks to Jake."

"No. Thanks to Jake you still get vertical every day." Jamal took a sip of coffee and let it sink in. "Besides, when you have all that department brass inertia behind you…well, it gets to be a bureaucratic runaway train sometimes."

He had a point. The case ended up going exactly the way Management wanted it to go. And I'm the one that got reassigned.

"Here's how it works. I can get places—I can talk to people—I can ask questions that might get certain folks with, you know, official public duties into a heap of constitutional trouble."

I nodded.

"I don't need—or want—official file information that's off limits. Sometimes a little space helps. Time is good, too. A wink. A nod…a point in the right direction."

"If you already have this understanding with Jake, what do you need me for? I'm just on temporary duty in his world."

Jamal sighed, sat up straight, and leaned in towards me. "He's on a bad path and, frankly, I'm worried."

"Bad path? How? What does that mean? Him and me?"

"No. No, professionally. This case is starting to lead down some dark rabbit holes, and the feel is, well, it feels like it's getting personal."

"You think Jake has too much invested in this one?"

"No. The Baron does."

The street sweeper android in the Muni Lot garage came to mind. Jamal was right. I found myself slowly nodding, and we came to have an understanding.

~~~

Windtalkers

After Jamal left, I lingered over a second cup of coffee and pondered. Some unnecessary filing was in order along with the straightening up of my desk. Then a third cup. I was in no hurry to get down the alley for Q's briefing, and by the time I got to the ACU conference room, no time was left for idle chit-chat with the gang—just the way I planned it.

I sat at the far end of the table from Q at the front of the room. Jake was up and across from me. EC was on my side, talking up a twenty-something female I hadn't seen before. Another androgynous analyst entered the room and reluctantly took the empty seat next to Jake.

Q got started with the same slide of unsolved area crimes from last time, reciting the basic facts of the cases, only this time connecting them to past crimes highlighting similarities in means, motives, and victim profiles. EC and the two analysts followed along on their *iSlates*. Jake and I focused on Q and the slides projected on the stark white wall behind him. Funny…you gotta look up every once in a while to see what's actually going on around you—especially if you want to be the kind of detective that closes cases.

Q droned on, reviewing my Ripper killings of prostitutes, the Torso Murders and, of course, the Sheppard case in Bay Village. I noticed Jake's gaze drifting off. Q talked about

Nightstalkers, Zodiacs, and the Son of Sam. I'm sure Jake knew all about them. Most of it was news to the rest of us.

"What's he like?" Jake suddenly asked out of nowhere, derailing Q's presentation.

"Who? Berkowitz?"

"Nah. Our guy."

Q was obviously stumped but didn't actually sputter out loud. EC and the analysts looked up from their *iSlates* at Jake.

"Really, how should I know?" Q finally asked.

Jake cracked a sly smile. *"Sympatico…No?"*

Q winced.

"Come on. The Baron isn't just some garden variety hacker. Neither are you." Jake watched Q try to shrug him off. "Code within a code within a code. A *Windtalker.*"

"Windtalker?" EC asked.

Q blushed. He looked at Jake. "So, cruising the Darknet, eh?"

"Everyone needs a hobby. So, where does he come from? Gaming? Tech? AI? VR? Spook Central?"

"Bored rich kid?" Q asked, staring down Jake.

"Yeah. Or bored rich kid." Jake nodded and met Q's stare.

"Anybody's guess."

"No. Actually, it is our guess to make. That's how we find this guy."

"He's kind of like an inverted profiler," said the analyst next to EC, drawing all the eyes in the room to her. She took a moment to absorb everyone's gaze. "I mean, no matter where he hangs, he's sponging up the lives of these killers and slowly squeezing them back out, drip-by-drip. Right?"

Nods around the table.

After a long pause, Jake asked, "A cop?"

"Uh…maybe?"

Jake sat back, clasped his hands together, and looked up at the ceiling tapping his index fingers against his chiseled profile.

"I-I don't mean—I don't really know. I'm not—*Not you, of course,* or…" She looked nervously at EC next to her.

EC laughed out loud. "Jake? Write code? Only with a number two pencil and an Agent Zero secret cypher wheel."

"Samantha's right," Jake said, leaning back into the table. "One way or another, it's an inside job. No reason law enforcement is off the table."

"Every family has its black sheep, huh," I said.

"Every serial killer had a mom and dad," Jake answered.

"Behavioral Sciences?" EC asked.

"Hell, no." Jake punctuated his objection on the table with his fingers. "The Feds got their share of geeks, too, in VICAP and White-Collar Crimes—No offense, Q."

Q shrugged it off.

"We need to keep this in-house—in this room, as a matter of fact. We don't get anyone else involved." Jake looked my way. "Sands will be good with that, right?"

"As long as we solve the case and he doesn't get ambushed with a ton of bricks falling on his head, he'll back our play—for as long as he can anyway."

And with that, I could feel the ice break beneath my feet and I fell into the investigation. I was now fully part of it.

~~~

Animal Farm

"So, you're in." Jake blocked my path down the hall outside the conference room after the briefing broke up. "Really in."

A shrug.

He squinted and gave no ground. "I can tell. I saw it in there. Partners, again. I'm glad."

"What about EC?" Though, truth be told, waitress Amy involuntarily came to mind first.

"He's good. But he's not you. He doesn't have the old bloodline from guys like your dad and Cutty. That's what it's gonna take. You know that."

"He seemed quite smitten with Samantha in there."

"It ain't smit. It's love." Jake drew out the word "love."

"Good. Good for him. He deserves it."

"Yeah, he does. We all do." Poker-faced Jake.

"I gotta—"

"There's my long-lost partner." Sanchez's voice called out from behind Jake. "I'm beginning to think you might like it down the alley here."

Jake turned and watched her amble up, missing the wave of relief that no doubt washed over my face. But Sanchez caught it. I could tell by the way the corners of her eyes crinkled, suppressing a smile.

"Welcome to our little corner of paradise, detective," Jake

said. "This is a pleasant surprise."

"For you, maybe. Me—not so much."

"Can I buy you girls a drink? I can make some fresh joe."

Sanchez looked over Jake's shoulder at me. I rolled my eyes and gave my head a shake. "Thanks, but no. I need to borrow Ms. Madeline, here, for a few hours or so."

"What's up?" I asked, pushing past Jake.

"The ninth floor called us down about the Williams case. The search warrant came through."

"Really?"

Sanchez winked. "Yeah. Funny. The wheels of justice and all. Maybe we'll find the weapon."

"Sounds like fun," Jake said, but there was no mistaking the disappointment in his voice.

"Come on, *la roja*. I've got a patrol unit sitting on the place waiting for us. And we don't want SWAT to get all prickly on us because we left them biting their chain for so long."

I looked at Jake. "I'll call…I guess."

"Sure."

Outside in the alley, Sanchez smirked, "*El novillo* in there seemed a little sad. Poor Ferdinand."

"Thank you."

"For what? Doing my job?"

"Yeah. That."

Up on the ninth floor of the Justice Center, Sanchez and I watched the suits come and go as we waited outside Assistant Prosecutor McGinty's office. You can dress them up, but the same animal instincts are there beneath the tailoring—the ones that when misdirected cause predators to cross my path. He waved us into his office.

"Detectives." McGinty greeted us but did not get up. He surveyed the sea of manila on his desktop, looking for our warrant. "Nicely done, snagging our friend in traffic court."

"We caught a break," Sanchez answered modestly. "Guess he didn't want to lose his wheels."

"Yeah, well, it obviously doesn't take brain power to rise to the top of the felony hit parade," McGinty effortlessly snatched back his compliment. He found our warrant and held it out. I reached over and grabbed it, but he didn't let go right away, cracking a sly smile and a one-eyed squint that treaded perilously close to being a leering wink. Our history was thankfully brief and pre-Jake. "Here you go, *Detective…*"

I smiled as innocently as I knew how.

McGinty released the warrant. "I really want that nine millimeter to seal the deal."

"Yes, sir." Sanchez quickly answered for me and grabbed my arm to lead me out, before any blood was shed. She shook her head after we got out of his office, muttering under her breath, *"El puerco."*

I had to smile: Sanchez's *Animal Farm*.

Outside Marcus Williams' apartment building just off Detroit Avenue on the near west side, we put on our vests as the SWAT team huddled to draw their Xs and Cs in the dirt before bashing their way in. Ten minutes later, Sanchez and I followed their conga line into the second-floor apartment once the battering ram took down the door. The rooms were quickly cleared, and Forensics was invited up to the party.

Gloved up in latex, Sanchez went through the dresser drawers while I mined the bedroom closet looking for the pistol McGinty wanted so badly for trial. Digging through dirty laundry was never my cup of tea, whether in a sparkling clean suburban split-level or a Section Eight hovel—and from the stench in the closet, it had been a long, long time since Williams had been to the laundromat. I started stripping coats, shirts, and pants from hangers, carefully squeezing down all the pockets before tossing them into the middle of the bedroom floor.

"Well, well, well. One step closer," Sanchez said holding up a couple of boxes of ammunition pulled from the underwear drawer. "Federal, nine mil—just like the casings we picked up."

I nodded, turned back to the closet, took a deep breath, and dug into the clothes piled two feet high on the floor. I prayed, *Dear God, please let there be no rats.*

Nearly gagging on the stench of sweat socks and Nikes at the bottom of the pile, I came up empty-handed. *I'll bet synthoid feet don't stink.*

With an assist from a kitchen chair, I cleared the shelf up top. A shoe box held several ziplock bags of pills. Underneath was jewelry, probably loot still too hot to fence. I bagged it, tagged it and took it out to be logged by Bunny Suit Boys and added to the bin.

A couple of other boxes up on the shelf had mostly knick-knacks—lighters, reading glasses, photos, pipes, papers, paraphernalia, and a junkie kit—but also a couple of knives which were obviously weapons—three-inch blades or longer, one of them spring assist opening. There was a prison shiv fashioned from an Oral-B and cheap flatware, obviously a memento of his alma mater, Trumbull Correctional University. Bagged and tagged.

I added some t-shirts to the pile on the floor and, underneath, there it was, wrapped in a Cavaliers jersey: A Glock 17.

The Darknet

"Bingo." I held it out for Sanchez to see.

She nodded. *"El puerco* will be happy."

It felt good to find it. But it still took two more hours to finish searching the apartment. Snapping off my gloves, I couldn't wait to get home and scrub myself clean.

~~~

Scene of the Crime

A scorching hot shower helped scour one crime scene off me physically. Despite a big glass of Petite Sirah, another lingered mentally.

I nested into my sofa and swiped through the Baron's case files, pulling pics out of the murder book galleries to tile on the screen for comparisons. I don't know how long it was, but I was on my second glass of wine without getting anywhere when one of Jake's crazy theories came to mind. He was always making dubious claims so that half the time you wondered if he was just making stuff up to punk you. He swore there was some academic psych study done decades ago that demonstrated temporary Alzheimer's whenever a person walks through a doorway, thus explaining that sudden amnesiac feeling when you step into a room and end up wondering what you went in there to get.

He insisted the same thing happened with browser windows, but I always thought it was just a lame excuse for him to avoid technology. Truth be told, though, switching from window to window to window was inducing vapor lock in my brain. I soon found myself printing out pictures and shuffling them around me like big puzzle pieces, like Jake would do. I started to sense something connecting in the photos, but, try as I might, I couldn't force it into a coherent thought.

Coming back from the kitchen with a third glass of wine, I lost the hunch I felt, proving Jake's crazy theory. *Damn it.* All that was left was a feeling of *déjà vu*. But I *had* witnessed this scene before—dozens of times—coming home to Jake's apartment to find open books, photos, and official reports scattered about his living room like evidential tea leaves he tried to read to crack a case.

With a heavy sigh, I gave up and put on my favorite playlist of old crooners—Bennett, Cole, Krall, Jones, Sinatra—that Jake had hooked me on and watched the setting sun melt the night over the foot traffic on the street below my apartment.

I shouldn't have skipped dinner. I was out before ten and up an hour earlier than usual. Surveying the explosion of wood pulp in my apartment, I fought the urge to gather it all up into neat piles, hoping my hunch might return.

After jogging the throbbing ache out from between my temples, I showered, dressed, and headed downtown, but not to the House.

I parked down the block until the street lights went out before I revisited the crime scene—*my* crime scene, as both investigator and victim.

It was this alley in the Flats where Jake saved me…and lost me. *Literally.*

I stood back on the curb, staring down the alleyway into the lingering stains of nighttime darkness. I wish I could say I remembered what happened, but my memories of the attack are synthetic, just replays of the video Q had found on the Darknet, showing the assault on me through the eyes of my synthoid attacker. Maybe it was better that my point-of-view was lost.

The Darknet

My footsteps followed those I planted months ago. The body had been found by a Republic driver pulling in to empty a dumpster at four in the morning. At least he was paying attention and didn't run her over. I guess there are some sights that will disturb even a garbage man, though—and gruesome it was.

White female. Twenty-eight. Split open like a watermelon at a Fourth of July picnic. With her intestines pulled from her abdomen and wrapped around her neck—just like the other two…and, later, Jeffery, the perp in the case Jake was working at the time. He had started connecting dots that drew different conclusions than had been sketched out in my case.

Management liked the crazy, lone wolf angle and prefabbed a house of cards for the press around it. They didn't want to hear about a serial killer from two hundred years ago and a madman breathing life back into him with modern technology. I was beginning to have second thoughts—and not just because of my relationship with Jake—and those seeds of doubt brought me back down to this alley in the middle of the night to be attacked by the robotic puppet master we called "The Baron." Jamal was right. Jake is the only reason I'm still alive.

I stepped to the back of the alley where the dumpster sat askew to accept human waste. All evidence of Alice's murder was long gone, but I could see the outline of her body as it was preserved in the murder book gallery. What I didn't see, nor believed later, was the connection to Whitechapel in London. At least not until it was bruised into me by a synthoid when I came back to the scene of the crime at two AM for answers. Answers that didn't fit Management's party line. By then, though, I had drunk the Kool-Aid.

I looked back towards the street, and a memory flashed—my memory, not a mental screen cap of Q's video—of one hand raised…of the glint off a large knife blade…of a synthetic smile placed there by a fiendish programmer, *the Baron.*

I shuddered, then left quickly to swap this alley for *Exit Alley.*

~~~

Waffles and Death

I tracked down Q on his side of the Exit Alley building. Funny how environment mimics its inhabitants. Jake's bullpen was messy and gritty—dirty cups, crumbs, and crumpled up paperwork and food wrappers strewn about—like real life on the streets. The analysts lived in an antiseptic cubicle farm. No danger of reality with its pungent bouquet of odors intruding here. Q's office was in a far corner. He saw me heading his way through the glass front wall and met me at the door. The eyes always give them away. I didn't know what he was guilty of, but he was.

"Detective...?" Half greeting, half question.

I smiled. It's the most useful weapon of choice we have with men.

"This is an unexpected—though pleasant—surprise. How, ah, can I help you."

"How does it work? Can you explain it to me?"

"What? Explain what?"

"You know, how is this all happening? I deal in flesh and blood evil. There are mysteries, of course, but the templates are as old as the Bible."

"Sure. Come in." Q stepped back to let me enter his office.

Behind me, I sensed the attention of testosterone drawn my way, like metal filings to a magnet. I looked back over my shoulder, and all the male prairie dogs disappeared back down into their cubicle holes. I imagined Q's scowl their way when he closed the door. Still, it makes a girl feel good and brought a smile to my face, which I quickly suppressed.

"Coffee? Tea? Bottled water or anything?"

"I'm fine, thank you." Sitting down, I surveyed: a pathologically neat desk; a coaster beneath his sports water bottle—*seriously, a coaster?*—and Andy Warhol's Marilyn Monroe hung on the wall behind his desk. An abstract print of red, blue and yellow squares outlined in black hung off to the side drew my eye.

Q turned and looked at the print. *"De Stijl."*

"Hmmm?"

"The style. Neoplasticism. Mondrian. He's very spiritual."

I smiled. *If you say so.* "Is that you?"

"Yeah." He handed me the framed picture I had pointed at on the credenza behind his desk. It was a not-that-much-younger Q, padded and helmeted up, flipping a BMX bike. "I used to compete."

"Used to?"

Q shrugged. "Weekender now. Skateboarding. Parkour. Just for fun."

I handed back the photo and wondered why anyone needed three phones. They were all neatly lined up on the credenza. One was more than enough for me. I smiled weakly with an ever so subtle sigh. "How does he do it? How does he get to them?"

"You mean, how did he get to you?" Q echoed my question softly. It had pained him to show me the video of my attack that he found on the Darknet. But I had made him.

"The victims."

Q pulled his *Alphabit* from his belt and contemplated it, turning the module left, then right one hundred and eighty degrees in front of his face. He set it down gently on the desk between us. "People think the Atlas Grid is like a fine wire mesh—and compared to the old cell technology it is. Instead of a grid measured out in miles, we're literally down to a square meter, and that's fine enough to locate a specific human or a human-sized entity. Without triangulation."

"Like a synthoid?"

"Like a synthoid."

"So?"

"So, everybody thinks of it mainly as a one-way street: up. For tracking. For navigation. For the efficient delivery of XG comsigs. But Atlas is not really a fine, two-dimensional virtual mesh. It's more like a waffle than a window screen. It has depth, depth in bandwidth. Not much, but enough for the Baron to use it as a delivery system, too. That is what's new. And pretty scary."

"New?"

"Munchausen hacks have always taken place at the machine level. The hardware and firmware were chopped to override the RSHA laws, and code was embedded into the OS to execute—literally—the murder. Sometimes the code is memory-resident and the synthoid actively hunts the target. Sometimes it's a sleeper that gets triggered by algorithms in the BLC logic ladder—"

"BLC?"

"Biology Logic Control. It's what makes the synthoid artificially human. It synthesizes sensor inputs, location coordinates, and library functions, like facial recognition and emotional response protocols."

"So, the AnSub waits until it finds itself in the right place at the right time with the right human in front of it, then kills?"

"That usually works if the droid is a direct plant into the vic's environment. First generation hacks. Crude, but effective. That was Jeffrey's MO on the Councilman's son. Nowadays, they hack into the target's digital shadow and employ predictive algorithms, to make sure the Munchausen shows up at the right place at the right time. You know, like a pop-up ad for an item you had searched for or a restaurant you liked and once reviewed—when you just happen to be in the neighborhood. Nothing left to chance, really."

"And that's *not* the scary part?"

Q grimaced and contemplated the irregular grid of the Mondrian.

"Is that how the Baron found me?"

He turned back to me with such a serious look on his face that it literally aged him in an instant. His brown eyes pooled into darkness. He picked up his *Alphabit* with his left hand and gestured with his right for me to hand over my *iNode*. I did. He set them in the middle of his desk, grabbed one of the cell phones from the credenza and motioned for me to follow him.

At the fire exit at the end of the hall, Q tapped out some code on his phone and opened the door without the alarm going off. We stepped outside into the alley, and he slid his ID between the latch and the door frame.

"Why the cloak and dagger?"

"Eyes and ears everywhere. You know that, Detective, don't you?"

I nodded.

"You have to create your own confessional booths." He pointed towards the surveillance camera above us. "And it helps to know where the on-off switches are."

"Catholic school?"

"Saint Eds."

"Magnificat."

Q nodded.

"So, the scary part?"

"The street sweeper."

"Huh?"

"The one Jake took down in the Muni Lot garage. It was a freelance."

"So?"

"Remember, I told you that a Munchausen had to be created hands-on by modifying the hardware and firmware."

"Uh-huh."

"The Baron has developed a push technology to plant malware in any synthoid he wants to. That's what the street sweeper was. Bob and Puff didn't find any mechanical mods. Samantha didn't find any unauthorized firmware patches in the chipset. He somehow knew the exact Atlas coordinates and mainlined his code into the OS to have the droid start smashing headlights and windows in the parking garage. He never had to touch it."

"Is that how he attacked me?"

Q sighed. "I think so."

"But it's still using a machine to commit a crime, right?"

Q nodded slowly. "But do you know what the PSA population is?"

"No."

"Millions."

"So?"

"He never had to physically touch it. So now instead of each Munchausen being a one-off creation, specifically chopped for a target, they are all potential weapons—any of them. *All of them.*"

"Millions?"

Q nodded slowly. "And that one was a city droid, not a civilian."

"Which means?"

"Not all synthoids are created equal. There are the Three Laws for John Q. Public. And then there are other laws."

I could feel a knot tightening in the pit of my stomach.

"So, who called this meeting," Jake interrupted as he came down the alley towards us from the precinct house. The tone of his voice had a hard, sharp edge. I could tell he was working too hard to hold his poker face.

Q and I watched as Jake walked by and tossed me a set of car keys. "A fresh one. You drive."

I started after Jake, but Q held me back by the arm. "We need to be careful. *All* of us. Very careful."

I looked him directly in the eyes. Maybe it wasn't guilt, but a dark knowledge. I gave a curt nod. Q released me, and I followed Jake to the parking lot.

~~~

A Hillside Dump

The ride to the crime scene was deathly silent. Nothing personal. That was just Jake's usual way, an angry meditation to prep for facing down the grim reaper's handy work. I could have let the *Crown Vic* chauffeur us but driving gave me something to do. It was a short trip down the Shoreway towards Battery Park. We got off at West 49th Street, near the Parkview Nite Club, a blues club Jake used to haunt in his youth until it went too upscale for his taste. The collection of official vehicles with flashing lights on Herman Avenue made GPS unnecessary.

As usual, Jake jumped out and went right for the body before the engine was even off. I tracked down the patrol unit that was first on the scene to get briefed. The guys were responding to a call from Animal Control which got a call from an elderly dog walker who noticed a growing circle of buzzards overhead and called to get a presumed carcass removed from the neighborhood before it drew coyotes which surely, she feared, would have eventually turned their hunger towards her beloved Bichon. I spotted her easily, cradling her pet in her arms among the gaggle of gawkers pooling outside the crime scene tape. Even though patrol had taken her statement, I went to speak with her. I didn't expect to get much more from her—and I didn't—but sometimes it's more about "customer relations" than police work, and witnesses feel slighted if they don't get to speak with a detective. Something Jake had no patience for.

I checked in with the body snatchers from the morgue to confirm the body had not been touched. Funny how Jake's reputation still held sway. Everybody knew to stay well back until he was done with his preliminary survey of the scene. He always was pretty amazing at seeing things everybody missed—even me—like some Native American tracker reading broken twigs and shuffled leaves, following a trail in the forest invisible to us palefaces.

When I got to the top of the embankment leading down to the Shoreway, I was glad to be wearing slacks. Jake was already halfway down by the body. I paused to take in the view: the city back to the east, the lake, the crib five miles out, ore boats unloading, the empty Soapbox Derby track across the highway, the Whiskey Island Marina, the old Westinghouse building to the west where centuries ago they actually made batteries. Then I carefully scaled down the hillside to Jake. The coroner and a photographer followed me down, figuring it was safe or at least that I'd shield them from his wrath.

"Hey, Jake. Long time no see."

"Hey, Elvis," Jake answered the coroner. Not his real name, which was Woodrow, but because—as it was explained to me—he dressed in white and always announced his departure by saying, "The body has left the crime scene." An inside joke between the two. I still didn't get it.

"Pretty."

"Was."

The victim was a female with dirty blonde hair fanned out around her head like a halo. Maybe late teens, but I was betting twenty-something. She was on her back, naked except for modest teal panties—nothing fancy, probably from Kohl's or Walmart—with legs spread out. Her arms were up with the elbows out and her hands together above her head, kind of diamond shaped. Behind and between us, the photographer quietly worked the scene.

"Patrol guys said she was dumped here, but…"

"Obviously not," Jake finished Woody's sentence.

The embankment was steep enough that if the body had been tossed over the guardrail in a hurry, she would have rolled all the way down to the shoulder of the Shoreway. Instead, her body had been deliberately placed vertically against the hillside and carefully arranged.

"Strangled, huh." All eyes were drawn to the ligature marks on the neck. "Wrists and ankles, too."

"Maybe." Jake knelt down beside the body and pointed to the crook of the right arm. "Puncture wound. The only one I saw and too healthy-looking to be a junk hound. Make sure you test that blue ooze around the injection site. I'll bet it's some kind of detergent or cleaning fluid."

"Seriously? Like, what, *Cheer* or *Windex?*"

Jake just nodded. Squinting, he looked up at me. "This has got Bianchi and Buono written all over it."

"Who's that?" asked Woody.

"Serial killers from LA, in what? The nineteen seventies?" I answered, vaguely starting to recall details of the case from Q's briefing slides.

"Seventy-seven to seventy-eight."

"The Hillside Strangler in the media. But there were two. Cousins," I explained.

"They taunted the police by pointing the victim's bodies at City Hall." Jake leaned over the body and looked out between the ankles. He stood up slowly. *"Damn."*

We all looked that way. There, on the other side of the highway, in the deserted stands of the Soapbox Derby track sat a solitary figure, watching us. Too far away to tell any distinguishing features. After a few moments, he—*or it…*stood up, turned, and walked away.

"Damn."

E.J. Quick

"Well, well, well, if it isn't the vaunted fourth estate," Jake said when we got back up to the top of the hill by the *Crown Vic.* He pointed out Jamal standing on the other side of the crime scene tape.

"Wait—let me get my shocked-face out of the trunk and put it on," I answered. We ambled over his way. He met Jake's eyes, then mine, and gave me a wink..

"Detectives…" Jamal fingered the yellow plastic tape like he was testing the fabric of a fine suit. Unlike the concerned citizens gathered in worry over the evidence of danger in their neighborhood, he smiled broadly and had the casual air of a man out for a walk in the park. "And what, pray tell, has caused so many civil servants to congregate together here this fine morning?"

"And he fancies himself a *crime* reporter," Jake taunted.

"It keeps me on the streets and in as much trouble as I can handle," Jamal answered. "But, I'm guessing, oh let's see, a one-eighty-seven?"

"Lucky guess." Jake shrugged his shoulders.

I just folded my arms across my chest and watched the two of them play their little game.

"Hows about a little look-see?" Jamal asked.

Jake shook his head slowly. "Mmm. Or not."

Jamal threw out his lower lip in a classic sitcom pout. "But all the other kids…"

"All the other kids what?"

"They get to see." Jamal held up his *iSlate* and tapped the screen to play a video. We squinted out the sun and saw ourselves skitter awkwardly down the hillside followed by Elvis and the photographer to the body. It was a *déjà vu* moment.

"What the hell?" I blurted out.

"Meanwhile, out on the net…"

"Where's that at?" Jake asked angrily.

"Over on the dark side, I'm afraid."

Jake and I simultaneously turned to look at the now empty bleachers at the Soap Box Derby track. "Damn it."

"You think?"

"Had to be."

"Had to be who?" asked Jamal.

"Where's the host?" Jake demanded.

"A DI-7 channel chat labeled 'JtR-Overlords.'"

"What is that?" I asked.

"The seventh circle of hell, for the violent. You gotta admit, at least there's some sense of culture on the Darknet." Jamal smirked. "Not sure about the 'JtR' part."

"I am. *The Ripper.*"

"Well, whoever they are, they've got eyes on you, Jake." Jamal shot me a look.

Jake noticed, then asked, "What are you doing prowling the dark side anyway?"

"You think my only sources are *official* sources?"

Jake just shook his head wearily.

"So, what's on this channel?" I asked.

"It ain't *I Love Lucy*."

"Lucy who?"

Jamal heaved a heavy sigh. "I'm trying to relate to the Neanderthals among us." He jerked his head towards Jake.

"Huh?"

"Another redhead in his life. The channel is mostly rants, manifestos, and homages to, shall we say, the homicidal elite."

"Serial killers," said Jake.

"Let's face it, they are the cream of the creative crop when it comes to the criminal element. Hence, the public's enduring fascination, I suppose."

"You suppose…"

"Eyeballs, Jake. Eyeballs. Clicks and page hits still rule in my corner of the world, dude." Jamal looked from Jake to me, then back to Jake. "But, as far as I can tell, the real business gets done there behind closed doors and through secret passages."

"Can Q help?"

"He could try, but I'm thinking the secret handshake is a pretty closely guarded secret. By taunting you with this video, they've got to be expecting that the *authorities* would bring them under excruciatingly close scrutiny. But, hey, tell him to knock himself out. Meanwhile, I know a guy or two who might know a guy or two who aren't afraid of the dark."

"Black gamers?"

"Yeah, shadow warriors. They're always up for a challenge that goes off the board."

"Great," Jake grunted, looking over Jamal's shoulder at the herd of media vans lumbering onto the scene like wildebeests coming to a watering hole. "You want to stick around for my 'no comment' comment?"

"Nah. If it's mainstream, it ain't Quick. I follow my own angles." Jamal slid along the crime scene tape away from the techs setting up their tripods. Before he was absorbed into the neighborhood crowd drawn towards the camera lenses like pigeons to popcorn, he warned, "Be careful out there."

It took a moment to feel the heat of Jake's glare.

"What?" I turned to face him.

"You...*and Jamal?*"

"God, no. And you got some nerve—"

Jake laughed out loud and shook his head.

"What?"

"You and Jamal? *That way?* No way."

"What then?"

Jake stepped in close, into my space, but I stood my ground. He spoke in a soft voice so only I could hear. "Just be careful around him. Hell, I'm careful around Jamal. Snake handling one-oh-one. He can be a good guy, but he's still one of *them.*"

I followed Jake's eyes to the reporters heading our way from the news vans.

"And trust me, he has fangs...and they shoot venom when need be."

I nodded, and my inside voice said, *Thanks.*

Jake held up the crime scene tape for me and to the cameras said, "No comment. *No comment.*"

~~~

Amy

On the drive back to the House, Sanchez must have pinged me a half-dozen times. I ignored them and rode out the silence with Jake. He bolted for Q's office when we parked, and I went up the alley and found my way home to Robbery/Homicide.

"You've got a visitor," Sanchez said when I got upstairs, meeting me at the coffee pot before I got to my desk.

I looked over and saw Amy sitting in the chair beside my desk. Though her clothes were newish, she was layered up like a homeless person. I didn't have to ask.

"Patrol found her down in the Flats. Near *our* crime scene. Remember?"

I took a sip of coffee, then sighed.

"Are those jokers in ACU going to be of any help at all to us?" Sanchez asked.

"It's getting complicated."

"Complicated don't really help us, does it?"

I just shrugged. "What was Amy doing down there?"

"Didn't say. Didn't ask. Just got her a couple of donuts and figured I'd wait, since she took such a shine to you."

"Thanks."

I took a long sip of coffee and observed. Amy sat nonchalantly picking donut crumbs off herself, yet still attuned to her surroundings. The occasional odd sound or new voice caught her attention and a dismissive gaze, like a wary cat, then she returned to grooming herself. I caught myself smiling, thinking of Jake's semi-feral cat, Frank. I shook it off and went over to my desk.

"Didn't expect to see you here," I said, even though I did—eventually.

Amy shrugged.

"You didn't have problems with the foster family, did you?"

She shook her head. "No. They were nice—okay, I guess."

"Looks like they bought you some new clothes."

"Yeah."

"I'll bet the food was better, too."

"I guess."

I shuffled through the in-basket on my desk. "So…"

"There's more."

"More what?"

"Of them."

"Them who?"

"You know. The machines."

Amy got my attention. "What do you mean?"

"Down there. I know where they come from, too."

"Show me?"

Amy hesitated, then nodded quickly.

"Sanchez," I called out. "I'm gonna get Amy a hot meal and take her back."

"You want I should call her social worker to do that?"

Amy shook her head quickly.

I rolled my eyes. "Nah, I'll take care of it."

We left and rode down to the Flats. I crossed over the river and went down off Detroit. We slowly prowled the West Bank.

"There's one." Amy pointed to a homeless man shuffling along.

"How do you know?"

"I know. I don't know how, but I know. It's not one of us."

I cruised by and looked closely but could not tell. And why would they turn a PSA into a vagrant? "Where do they come from?"

"The other side."

I turned on Sycamore to loop around on Winslow to Center Avenue. We crossed the swing bridge to the East Bank.

"So, how come you bolted?"

"It's not my kind of neighborhood. You know, picket fences, cutesy dogs, husky suburban kids."

I nodded.

"Where do you live?"

"Out in the 'burbs."

"Oh." Amy sighed heavily, as if she were a mother disappointed in her child's grades. "Turn down there."

I took a right. The flesh on my shoulders and back began to tingle. We were near the alley where I was attacked by the synthoid. Where Jake saved my life.

Amy watched me closely. "What's wrong?"

I tried to smile. "A bad night a little while back."

"Must have been really bad."

"Yeah. Yeah, it was. I'm lucky to be alive."

Amy reached over and gently put her hand on my shoulder. I didn't realize I had started shaking, even though it wasn't chilly.

"I had a case—cases, actually, where women were being murdered down here in the Flats."

"I remember. I knew one of them. Helena was always nice to me. Helped me with spare change whenever I saw her. Did you catch them?"

I bit my lip at the thought of the fiasco the case had become, putting me in my present situation with Jake. Then, it struck me. "Them? What do you mean *them?*"

"Stop. Pull over here."

I did.

"There." Amy pointed through the windshield to a three-story abandoned building down the street a ways. "They come and go out of there."

We were less than three blocks from the alley. I pulled out my *iSlate* and mapped our exact location: Ox Bow Bend, a particularly dark corner of the Flats, a graveyard of gritty businesses. I pulled the building's address and pinged it to Sanchez for a utilities check.

"Tell me."

"I sometimes come down to that old park under the tracks. You know, away from the bars and the sailors and what goes on over there. It's mostly quiet. And there's spots I know where it's safe, but you can see well enough to still keep a lookout. People are always going in and out of that place at weird times. And not like they have, you know, regular jobs or anything."

"Different people?"

"Um, yeah. A few different people. Sometimes it's hard to tell from so far away. I don't ever get close. Different vehicles for sure."

"Cars? Vans? Trucks?"

Amy nodded.

"The robots?"

"Yeah. You mostly see them come out and leave."

Sanchez answered: Minimal gas and some water usage, but a whole lot of electric going into the building. *Why for?* She texted.

Later, I answered.

Amy and I watched the building as dusk fell. No one came or went. The lights inside never came on.

"Come on. Let's get something to eat and get you back."

Amy sighed, then slowly nodded.

"What did you mean, did I catch *them?*"

"I really liked Helena," Amy sniffed.

"I know, hon. I know."

I put the car in gear, and we headed out of the Flats to the 'burbs.

Exit Alley

I went straight home after I dropped Amy off in the cookie cutter housing development in the Heights. The foster folks were nice enough, but she was right: it was a fish-out-of-water situation compared to living on the streets in the Flats. Of course, if Amy stuck it out, she would no doubt be running the neighborhood yard apes like some middle school *mafioso* don.

I was looking forward to an adult beverage before turning in when I remembered Sanchez and I were scheduled to testify at the Marcus Williams preliminary hearing the next day. So, I skipped the glass of wine and reviewed our reports. The case was pretty fresh in my mind, but if you slip up on even the stupidest little detail, the defense jumps all over it, and the grief rolls quickly downhill from the prosecutor's office through the command structure to Lt. Sands, who dutifully does his management obligation and delivers the corporate lecture on professionalism, case closures, and conviction rates. Besides that indignation, I just hate getting bested by the suits—especially by the off-the-rack guys in the public defender's office.

I met Sanchez the next morning at eight-thirty outside the Part B Felony Courtrooms.

A couple minutes later, McGinty strolled up. "Good morning ladies. Ready for this morning's show?"

"Mmm-hmm," answered Sanchez, dismissively looking down the corridor.

"Who wants to go first?" When neither of us answered, he went into playground mode. "Eeny, meeny, miny, moe—"

Sanchez's head snapped around so hard to deliver an angry scowl that McGinty actually took a step back.

"Right, then. Maddie it is." He turned on his heels and quickly entered the courtroom.

"I don't like that guy." I swear I could hear Sanchez's teeth grinding. She handed me the casebook with all our reports and paperwork. Although everything is digitized, of course, we still use a binder full of paper when we testify, so judges and jurors can see that there are real reports, real pictures, and, hence, real evidence against the perp. McGinty's right: it is a show.

"Yeah. Me neither. Let's start a club."

"I'm sure recruiting members won't be a problem."

"On either side of the blue line."

Sanchez answered with an angry huff and parked herself on the bench beside the courtroom door. She pulled out her phone and started swiping furiously at the screen. I sat down beside her and held the casebook on my lap, working to clear my mind to testify.

"So, what was up with the utilities on that place in the Flats? They use a lot of juice."

"Yeah, especially for a place that gives all appearances of being abandoned."

"What gives?"

"Amy said there's irregular activity—trucks, people, and synthoids coming and going at odd hours. Well, the synthoids mainly go."

Sanchez groaned. "Oh no, not Jake stuff. I don't like it. I don't like them. Don't know why anyone wants one of those creepy machines hanging around their house."

I nodded.

"Is this going to help our case?

Treading lightly, I sighed and said, "Maybe. You can't ignore the coincidences. And, after all, the vic was a Munchausen guy himself. Killed the lawyer in Jake's last case."

"Yeah, I read the DD-5s on that one."

"What the reports didn't say is that Jake thought all along he might have been involved in the Steinmauer murders."

"Your big case." Sanchez shook her head. "So, you think they turned on one of their own?"

"Who knew those guys were organized?"

"Maybe they get better benefits, being unionized."

The bailiff pushed out the courtroom doors and motioned me in. *"Showtime."*

"Knock 'em dead."

The bailiff stepped out and held open the door for me. I walked down the center aisle, got sworn in, and took the stand. McGinty made me wait while he went through the show of shuffling folders on the prosecution table. I never look at the perp. No sense in starting a staring contest, which sends the wrong impressions, like I'm out to get them personally. I'm just there to do my job. Like Jake says: Just the facts, ma'am. Just the facts. So, I scanned the gallery with a purposely disinterested look on my face, and something caught my eye, but—

"Could you state your name and badge number for the record, please?" McGinty finally got the ball rolling, and I turned my attention to him. His questions walked me step-by-step through the elements of the robbery and assault, taking the victim's statement at the hospital, canvassing friends and neighbors, and the arrest at traffic court. Pretty dry stuff, but again, no outrage, no hatred, no emotion. Just facts. "Was a search conducted of Mr. Williams' apartment?"

"Yes. Detective Sanchez and I executed a search warrant after his apprehension."

"Did you find any items related to the crime?"

"Yes. We found a Glock 17, Gen X, and boxes of nine-millimeter jacketed hollow point ammunition. Federal brand."

McGinty walked back to his table to retrieve the firearm. As he attended to the process of showing it to the defense and having the court enter it into evidence, I rescanned the gallery. Again, my eye was caught. A man in the back, wearing a Tribe baseball cap and lightly tinted glasses, sat watching me intently. I reflexively began to catalog his features and vitals, but it was too vague. Caucasian. Male. Age was, what? Twenty-ish? Thirty-ish? He pulled at his ear, and in that programmed motion I realized: he wasn't human. It took off the glasses. Even across the courtroom, the eyes appeared cold and reptilian. I shivered.

"Is this the weapon you and Detective Sanchez found at the defendant's apartment?" McGinty resumed his questions, holding the gun out towards me.

"Huh?" I took the pistol but looked over McGinty's shoulder. The synthoid rose, put the tinted glasses back on, and left the courtroom.

"Detective?"

I looked down at the Glock, cold and dark like the synthoid's eyes. "Ah, yes, well, this is a Glock 17."

"Detective…"

"Excuse me." I set down the pistol, grabbed my phone, and pinged Sanchez: *Follow him. B-ball cap & dark glasses.*

"Detective!" the judge barked at me.

The defense attorney sat up and suddenly started paying attention.

"Sorry, your honor." I picked up the Glock again. "Is this…"

McGinty approached the witness stand and stared me down. "Is this the weapon you and Detective Sanchez found at the defendant's apartment?"

"Let me be sure." I paged through the case binder and found the inventory sheet. I checked the gun, then the sheet. "Yes, it is. The serial numbers match."

The defense attorney sighed and shook his head.

I looked down the aisle at the doors leading out of the courtroom and wondered if Sanchez got my message in time.

McGinty's questions continued to lay out the details of the state's case against Marcus Williams, but my thoughts were outside the courtroom. McGinty, taking note of my distraction, silently questioned the judge with open palms and a raised eyebrow. The judge gave a single sharp nod of his head. "No more questions."

"Defense?" asked the judge.

"No questions, your honor."

"The witness is excused."

I quickly gathered my things up.

"Mr. McGinty?" the judge asked.

As I quickly made my way out of the courtroom, McGinty and the judge went through the script of binding the defendant over for trial.

Sanchez was gone. I called her but got no answer. I called the desk sergeant to check her Atlas Grid location. Sanchez was down in the Flats. The sergeant sent me her track. I ran to the car and followed her down. By the time I got to the alley where I had been attacked by the synthoid, her dot on the map had not moved for twenty minutes.

I took a deep breath and approached the entrance to the alley. Peering around the corner, I—she was there on the ground, lifeless. I drew my weapon and entered the alley.

"Oh, Rosa." Her body was clearly broken, but she was barely breathing, so I made the call. "Officer down. Officer needs assistance."

I gave my location and moments later I heard sirens.

~~~

Whitechapel

I stayed glued to Sanchez's side, holding her hand, until the EMTs rolled her away. Then, Jake ushered me out of the alley. I didn't even realize he was there but should have known. It would be an ACU case.

"It should have been me. It was there—in court. They're stalking me…or maybe all of us. Who are these guys?"

Jake didn't answer. He just kept his arm around my shoulders as we walked down the dirty sidewalk in the Flats, away from the crime scene.

I stopped and turned to him. "Who are these guys?"

"Not here." He pulled me along. "We've got to be careful."

"Why? What's wrong?"

He leaned into me and whispered, "They're unlatched. *Free range,* Q called it. They're not on Atlas—and yet, they are. Black data pipes or something."

"Waffles."

"Huh?"

"It's how he described it to me."

Jake nodded.

"Come on." I led him away from the crime scene, further into the Flats, heading towards Ox Bow Bend, the park, and the abandoned building Amy showed me. We cut through the park and followed the curve of the river until we got to the train tracks overhead. I pulled Jake behind one of bridge supports and pointed. "That one."

"Yeah?"

"Sanchez said it's sucking in more electricity than the lights at an Indians night game."

"What's inside?"

"Vacant. Records show it's owned by White Chapel Associates, LLC."

Jake gave me a quizzical look.

"What?"

"Whitechapel?"

"Yeah. So?"

He shook his head. "It's them. Right under our damn noses."

I nodded.

"Is that why Sanchez was down here?"

"No. I was in court, and I saw a droid in the gallery. When he left, I had her tail it—" I bit my lip. "Maybe…"

"Don't go there. It's not on you." Jake stroked my cheek, then squeezed my shoulder. "Let's get out of here before we attract anyone's attention. I'm sure they're camera-ed up."

"I should head over to Metro to check on Sanchez."

"I'll collect EC, and we'll come back down here to put eyes and ears on that place."

Once back at the crime scene, we went our separate ways, again. Jake sought out his partner, and I went to check on mine at the hospital.

~~~

Metro ER

The automatic doors whooshed closed behind me. I scanned across the sea of human pain of those awaiting triage and absorbed the salty odor of sweat and fear and antiseptic. I got to the ER too late. Sanchez's family—her sisters and mother—were sobbing with quiet dignity in an out-of-the-way corner of the crowded waiting area. A uniformed officer stood guard to protect their privacy until Management could get there. The pained look on the officer's face read out like one of Q's PowerPoint slides. I couldn't help but understand: Sanchez was gone. The muscles in my shoulders tightened. I closed my eyes.

The firm grasp on my arm sent a wave of relief over me; I was grateful that Jake had come. I slumped back into the arm around my back, but when I opened my eyes, it was Jamal. I stiffened reflexively, but he just smiled and nodded.

"Come on. Over here." He led me away from the Sanchez family to an empty corner of the waiting area.

"I should…" I looked back over my shoulder.

"In a minute. The doctor just left them."

We sat down side-by-side. I took a few deep breaths. Grief and anger mingled as I struggled to bring my thoughts into some kind of order. But all that came together was a question: *Where is Jake?* I really needed him there.

"Can I get you something?"

Jamal's question brought me back to the moment. I must have looked at him like he was talking at me in Mandarin. It made him chuckle. "Coffee. Please."

"Black, right?"

I nodded quickly. I just wanted him away for a moment.

"Be right back."

Jamal left. I stared across the ER, wanting to go to them, but unable to stand. My hand found my shield on my belt, grabbed it, and held onto it hard. I don't know how much time passed before the aroma of freshly brewed coffee drew my eyes to Jamal standing before me. I took the cup, blew over it, then sipped carefully.

"Thanks."

He sat down again beside me.

"It was the same alley," I said.

"I know. That's why I came." Jamal leaned forward and rested his elbows on his knees. He looked straight ahead. "It was one of them, right?"

I nodded, then sipped to mask my guilt.

"What was she doing there?"

"She followed it from the courthouse."

"Huh?"

"We were there for a hearing on one of our cases. I was testifying and noticed a synthoid in the gallery. When it left she followed it and…"

"In the gallery?"

I nodded.

Jamal sat up and looked at me. "That's strange."

"Why?"

"How did it get through security?"

The Darknet

I frowned.

"They don't let civilian PSAs into the Justice Center."

"Oh, no…" My hands began to shake, sloshing coffee on the floor. Jamal grabbed the cup out of my hands. "Excuse me."

I got up and bolted towards the entrance doors with such urgency faces turned my way like the wake of a speedboat cutting through water. Outside, I ran to the far end of the parking lot. Leaning on a stranger's car, I caught my breath and called Jake. He didn't answer, so I called Q and told him to get down to the Justice Center and inventory all the synthoids there. I don't know how many they had, but I was sure one was missing.

Across the lot, I saw Lt. Sands, Captain Caldwell, and a Public Relations guy pull up and enter the ER.

When I went back in, Jamal was gone.

Media Glare

We were in an empty patient room, standing on opposite sides of the unmade hospital bed. I briefed the PR guy, and he left with his notes. Wordlessly, Lt. Sands asked the Captain for the room.

"You've got three minutes," Caldwell muttered, checking his watch. "I want to go live at the top of the hour."

Lt. Sands nodded, then sighed.

I stared at the middle of the bare mattress.

"What's going on, Maddie? What's really going on?"

"They're coming after us."

"They who? What us?"

I shrugged. I wouldn't have believed it either a week or so ago.

"Maddie..." His voice was calm, friendly—not his briefing room command voice or his scolding Management tone. "You know this is going to go ugly...fast—like three minutes fast."

I nodded. "We don't know who, exactly, but we do know where. In the Flats. At least it's a good lead."

"Jake?"

"He's down there now. With EC. Setting up surveillance." I could feel my breathing quicken. "They're sick, serial killer wannabes."

"You keep saying *they*. Munchausens?"

I looked up and slowly nodded. "Only worse. It's like a dark gaming cult or something—I don't know exactly."

"And they came after you?"

I nodded.

"And Sanchez?"

I bowed my head and couldn't stop myself from letting out a muffled sob. *"Damn it."*

Lt. Sands reached over and squeezed my arm.

The door opened, and the PR guy stuck his head in. "You guys have got to get out there. *Now.*"

Lt. Sands looked over his shoulder, and the suit disappeared like a groundhog seeing his shadow. He turned back to me. "You want out?"

I shook my head.

"Didn't think so. Come on."

I walked around the bed.

Lt. Sands put his arm around my shoulders and walked me to the door. "Let's get through this. Then get those SOBs."

He held the door open for me, and we slid along the wall down the hallway crowded with media types to join the Captain and the PR guy facing a bank of video cameras and outstretched cell phones. Sanchez's sister, Lorena, stood next to the Captain. She shot an unfriendly look my way. I couldn't blame her. If I had been with my partner, Rosa wouldn't be dead. I hung back a bit, just behind Lt. Sands' right shoulder.

It hadn't been that long since I had been in the center ring of the media circus when I solved the Steinmauer serial killer case—or thought I had. Everybody did. Except Jake—and he was right. I was the hero back then, but that screw was sure to turn. Reporters have long memories.

"Good afternoon, everyone," the PR suit greeted the reporters. He went through the "who, what, when and where" of what happened to Sanchez. Then he gave a brief summary of her service and turned the stage over to Caldwell. I tried not to squint at the glare of the lights, but I wasn't as practiced at it as the Captain. He consoled Lorena and expressed an appropriately measured rage at the loss of one of his own. I know it played well. I had seen it before, only now, for the first time, I was on the wrong side of the news, especially when they can knock someone down a notch or two.

Lt. Sands stepped forward and vowed to find the killer or killers, then asked for the public's assistance. When he finished, questions erupted from the crowded reporters. Off to the side, in the back, I noticed Jamal. He wasn't taking notes, just watching.

"Detective, where were you when your partner was murdered?" It was Kirstie from Action News 5, claws exposed.

I tried to step forward—I couldn't let silence be my answer, but Lt. Sands held me back. Thankfully, the PR suit ended the press conference.

Jamal shook his head and quickly left.

Uncle Cutty

I wanted badly to use my lights and siren to plow through all the traffic to get back to the House ASAP but didn't. When I got there, I went straight to the ACU in Exit Alley. The detective's bullpen was empty. On the other side, Q's office was dark. The techs all stayed hunkered down in their cubicles. The tapping of keyboards slowed to a weak, erratic trickle, like the spooky ticks of an abandoned old house. Scared little rodents, waiting for the cat to move on.

I went back out in the alley and took a deep breath polluted by a nearby dumpster. I couldn't bring myself to go up to Robbery/Homicide, so I cut through the back lot and headed for the Justice Center with a vague idea of finding Q.

Halfway there, my determination began melting away inside. I veered off course to Cutty's Deli. Though it was close to dinner time, the place was less than half full. Breakfast, lunch, and shift changes were his busy times. Even still, the din ebbed as I cut through the tables towards an empty booth in the back where I could hide out. Word about the loss of my partner traveled fast. I slid into the booth with my back to the room and hid my face in my hands.

Eventually, the scrape of ceramic sliding across the tabletop made me look up into Cutty's craggy face.

"Here, Mads. It won't fix anything," he said, pushing a

coffee mug my way half filled with Scots Whisky. "But it don't hurt, neither."

I wrapped my hands around the mug and shivered.

He sat down across from me and slurped from his own mug. "Go on. Take your medicine."

I sipped tentatively as if it were piping hot. It went down harshly, then warmed me. Hoarse from the whisky, I whispered, "Thanks."

He answered with a curt nod. "It's not really a happy club you've joined. And it's not very big."

I looked down into the amber liquid. Both Cutty and my Dad had lost partners before they rode together.

"You should at least take the day."

I gave a one shouldered shrug. "But I—"

"Don't. Some just don't make it to the end of watch. Not for us to second guess. Or pretend things could be different."

I sipped.

"Go see your Dad. Family's good at these times."

I nodded but knew I wouldn't have to go there. He'd be at my place waiting. "Thanks."

Cutty raised his mug. We clinked and drank. My coughing made him grin. "You'll be all right, Mads. It'll be all right."

I smiled weakly.

Cutty stood up. "Take as much time as you need."

He took a loud slurp and headed back behind the counter. I sat. I sipped. When my mug was empty, I sneaked out the back and wandered up Ontario Street to sit in Public Square until the sun went down. I wanted the night to give me cover when I got my car out of the employee lot. I found the bench by the Soldiers and Sailors Monument where Jake and I used to people watch when we were partners—official partners—and waited.

Later, sitting in the dark in my car, I was tempted to go down into the Flats, but didn't. Instead, I stayed up top and drove across on the Lorain-Carnegie Bridge. I cruised by the West Side Market, then down to the Shoreway past Edgewater Park. I cut back up to Detroit Avenue. I didn't think I had any route in mind, but I ended up parked across the street from Jake's building. The lights were on in his apartment upstairs, and I wanted so badly to go up and let myself in like before—like nothing had changed.

But I didn't. I couldn't.

After a while, I pulled away and drove home to meet up with my Dad at my place.

Uncle Cutty was right. Family is good.

Heat Signature

Pounding on my door woke me the next morning. Late. After my dad left, I decided to get up early and run but didn't set the alarm 'cause I usually don't need it. It was after nine, though. I guess events and exhaustion caught up with me. I wiped my eyes to peer through the peephole. Jake stood outside, so I swung the door open. He grinned at me. I let him in.

"Shut up," I said, trying not to sound groggy.

"Sorry. Didn't mean to roust you out of bed before the crack of noon." He came close.

"Shut up." I didn't mean to, but I wearily leaned into him. He put his arms around me and held me. It hadn't been that long, but it had been too long. I closed my eyes and slowly squeezed him close to me. He let me. "Just shut up."

After a while, he kicked the front door closed with his foot. "Come on. Let's get some coffee in you."

Jake led me to the kitchen. I sat at the breakfast bar while he loaded up the coffee maker. He didn't have to ask. He knew where everything was, and it wasn't long before I had a steaming mug in front of me. The Columbian dark roast smelled great.

"I came by last night but saw Mac's car. I figured…"

"Yeah. He left about two." Dad liked Jake but hated that I got involved with another cop. "He was going to crash on the couch, but I talked him out of it."

"Good call. It's a killer on the back."

I smiled. Jake might have spent one night on the couch, the first night he ever stayed over when he came to me after his suspension. "What did you and EC find down in the Flats?"

Jake held up his hand and shook his head. "Um…maybe you should get dressed, and we can take a walk. Go down by the pool."

I could feel myself blushing. All I had on was my Forty-Niners jersey. "Yeah. I'll, ah, be right back."

"No hurry." Jake tossed a leer my way. "Finish your coffee."

"I'll be right back." I hopped down off the stool, grabbed my mug, and marched back to my bedroom. I slammed the door closed for effect. I dressed in shorts and a tank top to torment him, then quickly dragged a brush across my teeth and, not wanting to deal with it, I just put my hair up. He said, "Go down by the pool," so I slid on flip-flops. Padding back out to the kitchen, I called out "What's going on at the pool?"

"A little privacy. No electronics." Jake took the *iNode* off his belt and set it on the counter with his phone. "And, you know, synthoids don't swim."

It brought me up short. I never thought about that. "So, you came by on official business."

"I came by last night—*unofficially.*"

I remembered parking outside his building the night before. "Thanks. I appreciate it. I really do."

We filled our mugs and headed down to the pool. What were they going to do? Arrest a pair of cops for using glass poolside? Most of the early morning lap swimmers were gone to work, and it was still too early for the tanning crowd, so the only other person there was an older gentleman slapping the water as he crawled up and down the length of the pool. We grabbed a table on the opposite side of the pool and watched him finish a lap, then turn.

"Tough about Sanchez. I'm sorry, Mads."

"Cutty helped. I stopped by the deli. Dad, too."

"Good." Jake reached over and squeezed my arm. "Anything you need."

"Did you and EC catch her case?"

He nodded.

"Good. What did Q find out at the Justice Center?"

"Would you be shocked to learn that confusion reigns supreme down there? At least six PSAs are totally unaccounted for. Their shop is a mess, so they could be piled up in pieces parts or wandering aimlessly about the city panhandling—or worse. Of course, they don't keep any tracking logs on their movements, since it's a closed environment. So, basically, the whole herd is unaccounted for, except possibly on Atlas—presuming their firmware settings were up to code. And that's doubtful."

"So, it was…an inside job?"

"Yeah, well, you'd think so with security screening to keep weapons and civilian PSAs out of the Justice Center. But then again, droids have gotten through TSA at the airport, too."

I shook my head. "What about that vacant building?"

"Not so vacant. We put a FLIR gun on it, and it lit up like a four-alarm fire, confirming the huge electrical load. Q is pretty sure they have a serious server farm, but without an industrial strength cooling system, the plumbing probably can't keep up with it, so it throws off a pretty intense bloom."

"What's it for?"

"Well, the working theory was that Jeffery worm-holed NSA servers to download the Munchausen data packs into synthoids for his hits and keep them off the Atlas Grid. But Q could never figure out how he got in or out. And, you know, the spooks weren't going to be of any help—especially if you're pointing out vulnerabilities in their system. So, he developed an algorithm to see what he called 'free radical' metadata ripples in the grid."

I shook my head. "Techno mumbo-jumbo to my ears."

"Yeah. I still don't speak it fluently, but I've picked up some of the lingo. I mostly nod my head while Q prattles on out of my depth and get the English translation from EC later."

"So, what's the bottom line?"

"Are you kidding? The tech dweebs are always taking it to a next level, even when there isn't one, like it's all some big game."

"I think it is—to everyone but us…and the victims."

Jake nodded. "Well, this week's big idea is that they've found white space in the Atlas Grid bandwidth that they're using to push apps and libraries through, so there's got to be some serious computing horsepower behind it."

"Q's waffle theory?"

"Something like that. But me and EC are skeptical. Why would they go to all that trouble to stay off the grid, but be tied down to a physical location with a server farm that's going to tag them on smart meters? Plus, Q hasn't found any net port in or out of the place."

"What does any of this mean for what happened to Sanchez? And me?"

"I always thought that the attack on you was payback by Jeffrey. Now, I'm not so sure. And Sanchez…I don't know. It just can't be a case of being in the wrong place at the wrong time."

"Is this one guy? The Baron?"

"Unfortunately, the video on comings and goings at the building indicate it's a team effort. But there's got to be a leader of the pack. It's too organized. I'm beginning to think Jeffrey was a minion who went off the reservation when we got too close, so he became a loose end to be clipped—as well as a message sent to us. Q's been trying to infiltrate the DI-7 group, but hasn't been able to get past the gatekeepers."

"Have you told Sands?"

Jake shook his head. "Not yet."

"Anybody?" I stared Jake down. "Jamal?"

"No," he answered firmly. Jake started to say something else but stopped himself. He sighed.

"What?"

He shook his head. "Anyway, it's looking like our only move is to take down the server farm. If we do, we'll have no choice but to brief Management…and SWAT, of course."

"You really think tactical is the way to go?"

"The techies are coming up dry. Maybe we can get our hands on some real-world evidence before they get wise and close up shop."

We sat and watched the swimmer crawl through another lap.

"Take the day, Maddie. I can wait before I talk to Sands."

"Stay with me, please." My plea came out before the thought had even formed in my head.

Jake took my hand and squeezed. "You know I can't. The first forty-eight."

I nodded. The sun was warm, but the heat I felt came from inside.

~~~

Running Scared

I went for my run after Jake left to investigate Sanchez's murder. I prefer the cool of early morning. The day was heating up, but I thought it would still make me feel better, clear my head. Usually does, but it didn't this time.

Jogging up towards the entrance to the Metropark, a feeling of dread came over me. And maybe fear. I wasn't even halfway, but I stopped. Panting, I stared down the lane into the woods, shoulders tingling with a primordial, animal warning mankind never lost even after we crawled out of the evolutionary muck.

I tried to tell myself it was only an echo of the fears wrapped up in my initial reaction from the night before that it should have been me instead of Sanchez dead in the alley. My gut knotted hard, though—to a present danger, not a recollection.

Shuffling back away from the woods, I reached into my fanny pack and found a grip on my Glock 26. I pirouetted to scan all around me, then turned and ran back towards suburban safety, looking back over my shoulder every few paces until I reached the condo development. I slowed to a brisk walk, breathing hard, not so much from exertion as emotion. When I got to Crocker Park, there was comfort in the mid-day crowds of shoppers and workers breaking for lunch. I finally released the grip on my pistol and slowed my steps to blend in with the foot traffic. Still, it took a conscious effort of breathing deep to bring my heart rate down.

My feet found their way to the storefront bakery where I occasionally allow myself indulgence, as if they knew that returning to my empty apartment was the wrong thing to do just then. The clerk's unspoken impatience as I stared blankly at the pastries in the counter and the customers lining up behind me nudged me into getting a brownie and a cup of coffee, though I really had a taste for neither.

An empty bistro table on the sidewalk out front beckoned. Sitting down with my back to the shop, I could see up and down the street. Eventually, I took a bite of brownie. It made me realize how dry my mouth was. A sip of coffee did not help much.

"Detective…"

Though familiar, the voice startled me. Jamal had sneaked up on me as I stared into my coffee and stood on the other side of the wrought iron fence beside my table.

"Are you alone?"

I arrested my instinctive answer. A deep breath. "Just a little me time…and a sweet reward for sweating it out."

"May I join you?"

I glanced at the empty chair on the other side of the table and shrugged a shoulder. "Sure. Why not."

"Let me grab some java."

I had never encountered Jamal out this way, in the 'burbs. According to Jake, he hung out in grittier neighborhoods, closer to downtown, often in the Flats.

"Are you sure it's okay?" He stood behind the empty chair with coffee in hand.

I nodded.

The Darknet

"My condolences on your partner." He sat.

I nodded, but wondered at the comment, since we had spoken at the ER. I took a sip and peered over the rim of my cup. "So, are we talking on the record? Or are you stalking me on your personal time?"

He smiled. "Like rust, news never sleeps either."

I sighed. "I wasn't there. I can't tell you anything. You should probably talk with Jake. He caught the case."

"Um…definitely another Munchausen episode, then."

I involuntarily grit my teeth.

"First you…then Sanchez…"

The unasked question hung in the humid air between us.

"It's kind of hard to figure out what's going on, huh."

"We usually don't know until the very end. That's why they call it an investigation. And answers don't always come as easy in the real world as they do in Hollywood scripts."

"Still, for you to be on the receiving end of things. That's, well, highly unusual. Especially in ACU cases."

I kept my thoughts to myself.

"Anyway, Jake will get to the bottom of it, I'm sure. He's got a nose for it, even though he hates Exit Alley."

"He gives a hundred percent in whatever he does."

"I know. But he's got a blindside, too."

"What does that mean?"

"Careful, Maddie. Just be careful. It's a dangerous world out there." He took a long, loud sip of coffee.

"Out where?"

Jamal just smiled. "Sometimes it doesn't matter where, exactly, where is. Danger finds you."

Heat pulsed through me like a wave lapping the shore,

followed by a cold shiver. "Do you know something, Mr. Reporterman?"

Jamal cracked a smile. He casually looked up and down the sidewalk. "No. Not really. It's just the way it is. You should know that."

"She was my partner," I hissed.

"I know. I get it." Jamal sipped his coffee. "But I've got a job to do, too. You have your leads. I have mine."

"And…"

"*And*…when this is all over, I'll definitely have a story to tell."

"This isn't just a story. This is real. I'm real. And Sanchez is…was real."

"Oh, I know. Believe me, *I know.*"

Another heatwave.

Jamal stood up. "You be careful out there—Jake, too."

I watched the reporter saunter off, stricken again by the shivers.

~~~

Psycho

The next morning, I sneaked up the back way to Robbery/Homicide early—before shift change, when it was still quiet. I really didn't want to cope with the steady stream of condolences from everyone and anyone I might pass by on the way to my desk. I hate funeral receiving lines and have ever since my favorite cousin died in a sledding accident when we were thirteen. No doubt they would all be sincere and mean well, but…honestly, *déjà vu* twenty or thirty times over loses its charm and novelty quickly.

When I got upstairs, she was sitting at my desk—the woman from CPS. "May I help you?"

"Oh…Detective…I, ah, didn't expect to see you back at work." She stared blankly at me.

"And?"

"And, ah, I heard about Detective Sanchez. Sorry." Okay, not all of them sincere. She stood up abruptly. "I was just leaving a copy of the missing persons report."

"Who's missing? Amy?"

"Yes. She's been gone forty-eight hours. And I did file a report with the local police." She picked up a piece of paper off my desk and waved it at me. "I was just leaving you a copy."

I nodded. "Did they issue an Amber Alert?"

"Oh, well, I wouldn't know about that. I can only do what I can do."

"I guess as long as the paperwork is in order."

"I can only do…*What I can do.*" She gathered up her over-sized Naugahyde file cabinet stuffed with manila folders, her briefcase, and her purse. "You have the report. Good day."

I watched her trundle down the aisle between the empty desks. It was true magic that a mere eight-and-a-half by eleven piece of paper could cover that ass. I started to sit down at my desk, but my eye caught a glimpse of Sanchez's trinkets and family photos on her desk across from mine. I got a cup of coffee and sought refuge in Lt. Sands' office—for how long, I really couldn't say. I kind of blanked.

"Can I get you a warm up?" Sands asked.

Startled, I hopped to my feet, looked into my empty cup, and was relieved. I would have been wearing coffee otherwise. "No—I can—I can get it."

"At ease, Maddie. At ease. I'm going that way."

I surrendered my cup.

"You know you don't have to be here, yet," Sands said when he returned, handing my cup back.

"I know." I moved from the sofa to one of the hardwood chairs in front of his desk.

He sat down behind his desk and immediately began shuffling papers around. "You want in on the ops?"

I nodded.

"Yeah. I figured. The judge should be signing off on the warrant today. We meet with SWAT this afternoon, so they can do their mission planning thing. So, likely tomorrow. The earlier the better."

"And Sanchez?"

"Commissioner's office is handling the arrangements with

the family. It'll be a few days to put everything together. Line-of-duty death and all. It'll be a big deal."

"Should I…"

Sands shook his head. "Just lay low for now. Emotions are still running high. In fact, do yourself a favor and get down to Public Square. See the department shrink if you can. At least, get an appointment set up for your mandatory session."

"But I'm fine."

"Come on, Maddie. It's policy. You know that. Don't make it hard for me—or you."

I nodded. "Does Jake have anything?"

He shook his head. "It's early. But him and EC are dogging it."

I sighed heavily.

"Go on over to Public Square. Maybe you can put that behind you." Lt. Sands tapped a pencil impatiently on his desktop. I got the hint and stood up. "Besides, maybe hanging around the squad room might not be the best thing right now."

"I'll go." I threw out my lower lip. "But I won't like it."

"No one does." He shooed me out of his office. "Now, go on. I've got important police work to do."

Sands was right on all accounts. I went out of the House the way I came in and avoided well-wishers. Jake's car or his motorcycle weren't in the employee lot, so there was no point in putting off the department shrink by hanging out at Exit Alley. I thought about stopping by Cutty's on the way, but it would be jammed with the breakfast crowd. No reason to put a damper on that party, so I headed over to Headquarters.

Still too early for the bureaucrats in blue, I found a hole-in-the-wall coffee shop, grabbed a cup, and made my way up to the third floor where the medical staff was housed. Before I finished my coffee, the department psychologist showed up—even before the secretary.

He recognized me right away. "Detective…I wasn't aware the notification had gone out yet."

"Probably didn't. My CO recommended I come over." I stood up. "So, do I need an appointment, or do you guys take walk ins?"

His beard parted as he cracked a smile. "Sure, come on in. Though I have to say, usually it's like pulling teeth."

I flashed back my pearly whites.

So, I had a fairly pleasant conversation with the guy in his fairly pleasant, but bland, windowless office with the nondescript decor and framed family photos of a wife and a couple of kids that I swear were really characters from central casting. Or maybe they came with the frame. Mostly we talked about the job. Touched on following in my dad's and his dad's footsteps in joining the force. Talked about Sanchez, of course, but also Walker and Jake.

"Kind of unusual to have so many different partners in such a short a time."

"Yeah, um, I guess." I pondered. He had a point. "But, you know, Jake got punished for what he did—for what happened to the Councilman's son. Walker retired. And Sanchez…"

"Still…"

"But, you know, there's nothing I could have done about it."

"Still…"

I didn't know what to say.

"Do you want to stay in Robbery/Homicide?"

"I do." And I did.

"Even after what happened to Sanchez? After all, it's an ACU case."

"They'll take care of it."

"Jake?"

I nodded. He seemed to know too much about things.

Involuntarily, I let out a sigh.

"I have to ask." The psychologist took a deep breath. "Any significant changes in your personal life recently?"

How did he know? I asked myself. Then I realized that he already knew all about me and Jake—on duty and *off*. In fact, our entire conversation suddenly had a creepy, scripted feel to it. I nodded.

"Intimate?"

I nodded again.

"Male or female?"

I shot him a scowl.

"Okay. I get it. What happened? Was there someone else involved?"

I thought about waitress Amy and Jake being together. But that was before us, then after us again. I shook my head.

"What happened?"

I shrugged my shoulders. "I guess we drifted apart."

He stared at me, then finally said, "But he saved your life."

"You know about Jake."

He nodded. "So, what happened?"

I looked away, but there was nothing interesting in the office to look at really. "I guess I screwed up."

"How's that?"

Just then the phone rang. "Saved by the bell, eh." He got up reluctantly and went around his desk to answer it.

I listened to him listen and uh-huh his way through the call.

"I'll send her over." He listened. "Yeah. That would be best for now."

I sat up straight. "Me?"

"Your lieutenant. There's a briefing scheduled with SWAT in an hour or so down at…*Exit Alley?*"

"It's the Artificial Crimes Unit. It's literally a building down the alley from the House."

He smiled. "Huh. That's an…interesting allusion."

"It's filled with innn-teresting characters."

"Jake?"

I nodded.

"I'll fill out the paperwork, and you'll be cleared to return to duty after Detective Sanchez's funeral. It will take that long for my report to get processed. You'll get an official notification mailed to you. Modified desk duty until then, but I agreed with Lt. Sands that you can be there tomorrow—but only to observe, then assist after the scene is secured. Okay?"

I nodded and headed for the door.

"Maddie…"

I stopped and felt my grip tighten on the knob. *There's always more, damn it.* I looked back over my shoulder.

"Don't let it consume you."

"What? Sanchez?"

"No. The job. Don't let it suck all the oxygen out of your life, your off-duty life."

I paused, nodded, then left.

~~~

War Plans

Everybody was milling about the big conference room when I got there, sipping refreshments and chit-chatting in clutches of threes and fours: Sergeant Kovacic and his SWAT team in their battle fatigues; Captain Caldwell, Lt. Sands, and a couple of civil servant types in suits and ties; McGinty, his secretary, and one of his Assistant Prosecutors; Jake and EC in street clothes; Q, Samantha, and a couple of other techs, dressed like skateboarders. I hung back at the fringes and watched like a distant relative at a wedding reception.

Jake and EC eyeballed the SWAT team trading asides, no doubt cracking wise over their Hoo-rah attitude like they always did. Most of the SWAT Team were ex-military, of course, still craving that adrenalin surge from overseas. *Muscle memories,* Jake called it, for muscle heads. He saw them as a necessary evil, like his Glock. Glad to have handy when needed but kind of annoying to just be hanging around. I was tempted to join him and EC but, instead, drifted discreetly to the back of the room and sat down to lower my profile. Sands saw me, though, and gave a quick wink and a nod. EC gravitated over towards Samantha. She was younger but not by that much. I hadn't seen him smile like that for a while, not since he lost his wife. She smiled back a lot. *Good. Good for him.*

Jake followed EC over and punched Q in the arm. Jake

looked my way. and our eyes met. He smiled. Then, just as he started towards me, the Captain called the briefing to order, and everyone drifted into seats, pooling together in their respective tribes.

"Okay. Looks like the judge signed off on our warrant." The Captain looked at EC and nodded when he waved the search warrant in the air. "ACU will brief on the perps and what we're looking for. SWAT on tactical. And then we'll wrap up with CSI and Prosecutor McGinty. Okay…Jake, you're up."

When he got to the front of the room, we made eye contact. I felt myself smile a little. His face rippled with a pained expression, then went "snake eyes."

"You are all familiar with the so-called Munchausen murder-for-hire crimes. What we are investigating in this case is a series of pattern, or copycat, crimes that are being executed—so to speak—by way of synthoids."

The screen flashed on behind Jake with the crime scene photo of the victim from Huntington Beach, mirrored side-by-side with a black-and-white photo of a woman's bludgeoned and bloodied dead body sprawled on a bed.

"The Marilyn Sheppard murder case from 1954."

A series of paired crime scene photos appeared behind Jake as he spoke.

"The Torso Murders from the 1930s. The Los Angeles Hillside Strangler case in 1977."

Jake paused to look directly at me. He took a deep breath.

"We now suspect that the recent series of prostitute killings in the Flats is actually the first one."

I cringed at the montage of my victims on the screen. A few people turned in their chairs and looked directly at me. I felt myself blush.

"And that was a copycat crime, too?" Lt. Sands asked.

I knew that he knew the answer to his own question. My inside voice silently thanked him for pulling me back out of the spotlight.

"The very first serial killer: Jack the Ripper. 1888," Jake answered.

"But wasn't there DNA in that case?" The Captain asked earnestly. He turned to look at Lt. Sands. Evidently, he was not yet up to speed on how my last case had gone seriously sideways after it was supposedly closed. "Droids don't have DNA."

"It was synthetic," Sands answered. "Created in a genetics lab at the Clinic by the doc who had her husband Munchausened."

"But that case was closed when the hacker was found dead in the Flats." Suddenly aware that his ignorance was showing in public, the Captain gave the Lieutenant that "you just wait till your father gets home" look. "See me after."

I was not looking forward to getting an invite to that meeting.

"So…Jake…" The SWAT team leader's usual stone-faced visage cracked with a broad grin, obviously relishing Management making a fool of itself. "Who's the perp—what do you guys call him, *Baron Von Munchausen?*"

The SWAT team giggled like a Girl Scout troop.

A slide of Jeffery's eviscerated body on the street quieted the room again.

"A synthoid technician at the Clinic was the prime suspect in the Mullaney murder. We started to like him for the Ripper murders, but, alas…" Jake looked at the slide of Jeffery's body behind him to make his point. "Anyway, the *Baron* actually appears to be more of a murder club that meets up on the Darknet. We haven't gotten into the chatroom, but evidence we've developed IDs the warrant address as a likely part of their infrastructure for pushing Munchausen code out through the Atlas Grid."

"Darknet, *schmarknet*. We operate out here in Meatspace, you know, the real world. You can't cuff up an avatar. Or have you forgotten, Jake?"

Jake stared down Kovacic. "You know, if you don't like the answers, maybe you should think twice about asking the question—*Oh wait…*" Jake put his hands to his cheeks and looked around the room. "Did I actually use the word 'think'?"

Laughs and chuckles percolated on the non-SWAT side of the room.

"Careful, pal. Remember who's got your back."

"Ooooo…"

"Youch."

"Careful Jake."

"Burn—Major burn."

The room quieted back down. EC took Jake's place and briefed on the building in the Flats that Amy had led us to. Then, Q did his best imitation of a shuffling, swayback perp-walk to the front of the room.

"Nerd alert," sneered the SWAT team leader.

Q put his hand into his pocket. A moment later a phone dinged, and Kovacic pulled his out of his pocket.

"What the hell! Overdrawn? How the hell can that be?"

Q cracked a smile.

"Oh, Lester…Don't stop, please." A woman's voice with a sultry Asian accent came out of the commander's phone. "Don't…stop…Les. More. More, Les, More. *Oh, Lester…*"

Out and out guffaws from the group.

"Enough!" The Captain silenced the room. "Bunch of damn five years olds."

"So, from a tech perspective," Q began, "we are looking at a significant server installation within the building that we suspect is being used to create a shadow network in the white space of the Atlas Grid to connect to free-range synthoids."

"White space?" asked one of the suits with the Captain.

"Unused bandwidth within the spectrum allocated for grid operations. In the zettahertz range, to be precise." Q stared at the suit.

"Uh, okay. Thanks."

"Free-range synthoids?" asked McGinty.

"In the past, hacking a droid required physical access to the unit in order to both modify hardware—required to override the RSHA Three Laws—and to implant firmware, software, and code libraries to program the droid for the specific crime to be committed." Q looked back over his shoulder at the slide of the dead hacker's body. "Jeffery, here—bless his heart—found a way to plant his code remotely once he chopped the synthoid by worm-holing through NSA servers, which all have various plug-in points in the Grid. And after the Munchausen crime, he could purge it of incriminating lines of code. A novel approach, which keeps the unit itself clean of any evidence of hacking. But the process left metadata breadcrumbs, which we were able to use to track him down. And if we could do it, surely the spooks in Utah could as well. So, Jeffery ended up with his insides on the outside."

"You mean CIA wetworks?" asked a CSI tech.

"No, more likely by the Baron's group. No doubt to hinder our investigation, as well as send a message. At that point, we thought this guy was a lone wolf, but…" Q looked at the SWAT team leader. "The bottom line is that the most critical objective here is to preserve and secure the server hardware *intact*—you know, without any bullet holes—so these guys can be identified and apprehended—and more importantly so ACU can find and repo the synthoids they've hacked."

"Collateral damage happens," said Kovacic.

"Well, it better not happen to those servers," said Lt. Sands.

Sergeant Kovacic took his turn, going through the Xs and Os of the SWAT deployment, the timeline, radio calls, and color of the day. The CSI supervisor echoed Q's call for preserving the scene for evidence gathering. Prosecutor McGinty's canned "by-the-book" speech was like a legal disclaimer tacked on at the end of a TV pharmaceutical commercial and closed out the meeting.

I saw Jake looking for me, but gave him the sign and sneaked out quickly to avoid getting sucked into the Captain's conversation with Lt. Sands about my last case.

He knew where I'd be: Cutty's.

~~~

Jake and Me

Cutty brought a cup of coffee to me at the back booth. He didn't say anything. Just put a hand on my shoulder and squeezed gently, then went back behind the counter.

Jake came in a sip or two later and worked the room a bit on his way back to me, hitting a couple of beat cops and a suit I didn't recognize. He stopped at the coffee machine, poured himself a cup, chatted up a waitress, then joined me.

"You made the right move." Jake slid into the booth opposite me. "Sands hadn't dropped the big one on Caldwell yet. *You gots some 'splainin' to do, Lucy.*"

I nodded. "Yeah. But not now. Not yet."

"Uh-huh. Better to deal with it when there's some good news—like after tomorrow."

"Yeah. Tomorrow." I took a deep breath. "Jake, I need—"

"So, you heard about Amy, right?"

The first thing that came to mind was stupid, blonde waitress Amy that Jake was sleeping with. "Oh, Christ. Really?"

He gave me a one-eyed squint. "The kid. She went missing again from the foster family. I saw the Amber Alert."

"Uh…yeah…Her social worker stopped by this morning and told me. Left a copy of the report."

"Oh, you thought…"

"It doesn't matter what I thought."

"Mads, it does. It does matter."

The conversation had gotten clumsy—not at all like I imagined it in my head as I walked back to the House from the department shrink. I knew what I felt, but I didn't really know what I wanted anymore.

"I was hasty, you know, after the attack in the Flats and all. I went off on you and shouldn't have."

"You are a firecracker." Jake smiled, then suddenly reached over and grabbed my forearm. "Wait—wait a minute. Are you, like…making amends?"

My skin tingled at his touch and I gulped a breath.

"You saw the head shrinker, didn't you?"

I could feel heat rising up my neck. Damn it. *He knew me too well.*

"You got nothing to apologize for, Maddie. Nothing at all."

"You always stuck by me. Always."

"It's what partners do."

"I should have…"

"I didn't like it. But I understood."

"You didn't?"

"Still don't."

"But Amy?"

Jake sighed. "I shouldn't have left you hanging out there like that. But I didn't know what else to do or how else to stop it from coming down on you, you know? He would have kept coming and coming. I had to keep you safe."

"Yeah. Maybe you're right." But I wasn't so sure.

"He's still coming—or they are. We're still not safe. You know that, right?"

"I guess." But I was still thinking about waitress Amy, not

the case. And thinking what a huge mistake I had maybe made.

"We'll get these guys, Maddie. We will."

"I guess," I said, but didn't know if I believed it. "We'll see tomorrow."

"Yeah. You look tired. Go home and get some sleep. O-dark-thirty comes awful early."

"I guess you're right."

Jake stood up. "I've got to go iron my dress for the ball…You okay?"

I just nodded.

Jake leaned over, kissed the top of my head, and was gone.

The Bomb Squad

After the two AM final briefing, I rode down to the Flats with Lt. Sands. SWAT was already down there clearing the perimeter, setting up the command post, and taking up their tactical positions.

"Sorry I bolted yesterday."

Lt. Sands looked over at me and smiled.

"I mean, you know, leaving you high and dry with the Captain. He didn't seem happy."

"Eh, he never is. It's my job to run interference sometimes."

"Thanks."

"Oh, don't thank me yet. I'm not a magician who can make it all just disappear. We are going to have to have that conversation eventually. But maybe we'll have some mitigating good news after today."

"Maybe, but…"

"Hope for the best, but expect the worst."

"Yeah. Something like that. Anyway, thank you."

We descended down into the Flats on the East Bank and followed the river upstream to Ox Bow Bend, turning on Columbus Road where the SWAT command center van was set up.

"What's the Bomb Squad doing here?" I asked Lt. Sands,

pointing to their step van up ahead. "I don't remember them in the briefings."

"Don't know. Probably SWAT pulled them in. Just in case." Lt. Sands parked. We got out, put on our vests, and hiked towards the command center. We passed a couple of SWAT guys all dressed up in their battle gear. "I sure am glad these guys are on our side."

It's funny how darkness can cover so much activity. They went about their business in a deadly silent way. Kind of creepy. I slowed down as we passed the Bomb Squad van. "I'll be along in a sec."

"Don't be too long." Lt. Sands tapped the face of his wristwatch.

I went around the back of the step van. The doors were open, and an eerie red glow oozed out from within. Inside, a couple of bomb techs were gathering equipment to suit up. "Hi, guys."

I startled them, then they saw my vest and badge. "Oh, geeze, ah, hi, uh…"

Kind of jumpy for bomb techs, I thought. "I'm Maddie."

"Hi, Maddie." They both grinned that stupid boy grin.

"Missed you guys at the briefings."

"Yeah, last minute call," said one of the techs as he lumbered down out of the van carrying his "fat" suit.

It was my turn to be startled at the sight behind him of three powered-down synthoids stored along the side of the van. "Huh."

"Be nice to know what the hell's going on."

"Yeah. Yeah, it would." I backed away from the van. "Hope you guys aren't needed."

"That's what everybody says."

"Don't take it personal, boys." I smiled coyly and hurried to catch up with Lt. Sands.

I drew all the eyes my way as I slipped into the SWAT van and pulled the door shut behind me.

"Detective," said the SWAT commander as he turned back to the bank of monitor screens along the wall above the console. "Make yourself comfortable. The show's about to start—sorry there's no popcorn."

Of course, there was no place to sit and make myself comfortable, so I sidled up next to Lt. Sands and surveyed the monitors. Along the top row was a grainy feed from a drone angled off and zoomed in to avoid detection. The video from the three snipers' nests was much clearer, one being eerie green night vision imaging.

On the second row were the glass feeds from Jake and EC, next to the SWAT entry team's body cams. Each one was labeled by name with magic marker on masking tape. On the third row were street-level views of the building. It was dark, but then again, the windows were probably blacked out. Thermal imaging showed a couple of warm bodies on the first floor and what could have been pizza ovens at full blast on the second floor. In all of the briefings and meetings down in Exit Alley, I was never able to ever really get what it was that Jake and Q and EC and everybody called the Darknet, where the Baron and his minions met and plotted and played out their sick homages to the sickest of individuals in history. But there it was on the monitor, dark...foreboding...real—and filled with nothing but the evil intents of evil, evil men. Hidden down here in a dark, forgotten corner of the city known as the

Flats, ignored by citizens crossing over high above on bridges during their daily commutes.

I gasped at the hand suddenly on my shoulder. I looked. Lt. Sands must have seen the fear and worry on my face and read my mind. "They're not going in alone this time."

I covered his hand and gently squeezed. He was right. I was glad Jake wasn't going it on his own.

It was going to be what SWAT called a "shock and awe" raid to gain control of the premises as quickly as possible in order to preserve the server farm inside from sabotage. As I scanned all the monitors, a creepy feeling came over me that something wasn't quite right. I didn't know what. Suddenly, the camera view from one of the sniper's nest zoomed in and drew my eye. The familiar conga line of heavily armed men shuffled rapidly through the shadows along the front of the building, barely visible against its dark facade. The infrared view on the other monitor made them look like a glow worm. It stopped midway. A moment later, the thermal image exploded, and every other screen strobed as the first flash-bang grenade went off.

"GO-GO-GO-GO-GO," crackled across the TAC channel. The body cams fed dizzying flurries of activity. All I could see on Jake's monitor was the back of the SWAT team guy he was following.

A hot flash broke over me. More flash-bang grenades went off. Suddenly, the command trailer walls closed in and I felt myself starting to hyperventilate. I had to escape the claustrophobic feeling gripping my chest tighter and tighter like a boa constrictor.

Focused on the unfolding raid, no one noticed when I stepped outside. The cool air slowly sponged the panic away. I caught my breath, but unsettled at being alone, I gravitated back over to the Bomb Squad van. The techs would still be there, waiting to be called in, if needed, after the building was secured.

I saw in the back of the van that two of the three synthoids had been unloaded. I walked around front, where the techs had staged their gear and waited, watching the front of the building intently and listening to the radio chatter through their earbuds. They both looked my way when I came up beside them. They smiled at me with a lingering gaze, then focused again on the building.

It was much more peaceful watching from outside. Rifle-mounted flashlights flickered occasionally in the building windows like fireflies on a dark summer night as rooms were cleared. Intermittently, a dull thump was heard as another flash-bang was set off.

I took a deep breath and peered up into the night sky. Getting outside, getting out of the face of the raid, had a calming effect. The dread I felt inside the command center dissipated like mist in the dawn.

When I looked back down, I reflexively began inventorying my surroundings, scanning the Bomb Squads gear. Ruck sacks and tool boxes sat in a small mound next to a small tracked rover with cameras, sensors, and mechanical arms sticking out the top. Next to the rover was one of the synthoids in idle mode.

"Where's your other synthoid?" I asked.

"They're back in the van," answered one of the techs, not taking his eyes off the building. "You only need one. The other two are backups in case the first one gets blowed up good."

I had to find Jake; one of the bomb squad droids was M.I.A.

Without thinking, I bolted towards the dark building, drawing my Glock as I ran.

~~~

Hunted Hunter

I burst through the main entrance into a lobby dimly lit with backup emergency lighting. It smelled like explosives and body odor—the extreme body odor typical of the homeless who counted the time between baths in months. A small group of SWAT guys rounded up vagrants from the first floor and lined them up against a side wall.

"Jake—where's Jake? Where are they?" I asked one of the SWAT guys.

He pointed up. I ran down the hall to the stairway at the end of the building and took them in twos to the second floor. The stairwell door opened out into a huge room filled with racks and racks of computer equipment. Cables snaked every which way across the floor. Smoke from the flash-bang grenades hung in the air, and flashlights cut through the misty half darkness.

Suddenly, the overhead florescent lights came on. The room spanned the entire second floor. I moved into the room, scanning frantically for Jake in rows of equipment racks and at the indiscriminately placed desks and cubicles. The walls were a combination of whiteboard scribblings and layers of printouts, pictures, clippings, maps, and pages from books and magazines taped up in some kind of haphazard montage, meaningful only to whoever put them up there. A half-dozen guys who looked like they could have been on Q's team sat around a conference table with their hands zip-tied behind their backs. I took a second look to see if I recognized the bomb squad's synthoid.

Jake was at the far end of the room chatting with EC as they surveyed SWAT securing the room. I sighed in relief, holstered my pistol, and walked his way. Halfway there, I saw him pull out his phone. Whatever he saw made him draw his pistol and bolt towards the stairwell in the corner, catching even EC by surprise.

"Jake! Wait!" But he was already gone.

"Maddie?" EC asked as I ran by.

"Come on."

I drew my Glock and entered the stairway quietly. I listened. Jake's footsteps were above me.

"What's going on?" EC said slipping through the door behind me.

"One of the bomb squad droids went rogue," I whispered and pointed up.

The door on the third floor creaked open and slammed shut. I hurried up the stairs along the outside rail, following the sight line of my pistol. EC followed with his shotgun at the ready, pressed against his shoulder.

In the moments it took us to climb the flight of stairs, crashing and clattering erupted from behind the door. We burst through to see Jake being manhandled by a synthoid dressed in green-gray coveralls with the yellow letters "BDU" on the the back. The droid swung Jake into a row of filing cabinets with a loud metal crash. It thrashed him about like a rag doll.

EC aimed, but didn't fire. The shotgun blast would have hit Jake, too.

I aimed carefully and shuffled slowly forward, waiting for some separation between them, trying to ignore Jake's bloodied, blank expression. He had obviously lost consciousness. I couldn't wait any longer and fired. It was risky—head shots always are—but Jake always said a synthoid's center mass is invulnerable to standard service weapons.

The impact of five shots pushed the droid's head around and maybe shattered an eye socket. Five more to its knees swept it off its feet and into a tangle with Jake on the floor. In human form, droids have human vulnerabilities.

EC ran forward to pull Jake's lifeless body away.

I came up behind the bomb squad synthoid and emptied my clip into its face at point-blank range, flinging synthetic skin and composite bone fragments off like shrapnel.

EC came back and blasted off its legs at the knees with his shotgun.

We backed off and watched the robot writhe on the floor, blinded and crippled, reaching out mindlessly for Jake to finish the job.

Hearing our shots, SWAT spilled out of the stairway door behind us, pushing us out of the way and surrounding the synthoid, though they didn't seem to know what to do with the mechanical perp.

"Call for medical," EC ordered. *"Now!"*

I silently prayed as I went over to Jake's body. On the way, I picked up his phone and looked at the screen.

Behind the cracked glass a video loop played of Amy—street urchin Amy—sitting on Jamal's lap. Behind them was the city, lit up through a window of the building. The fear on her face was obvious as Jamal stroked her hair with one hand and rested a pistol in the other on her shoulder, a grin of pure evil on his face.

"Come on, Jake. Come on up and get me," Jamal's voice looped over and over and over

~~~

Exit Alley

It was a cruel irony that machines now kept Jake alive.

I rode with him in the ambulance. Sat by him in the ER. Waited out the hours during the surgery. Then stood outside the ICU and watched waitress Amy weep at his bedside. I went home and finally slept for the first time in days.

Two days later, I went back to the House but not to my desk in Robbery/Homicide. I found myself at the ACU offices down the alley…*Exit Alley*. Jake's exit.

The bullpen where the detectives had their cubicles was a ghost town. Jake's desk was like a crime scene that no one had taped off. Not even the cleaning crew moved his chair to sweep the carpet underneath. I just stared at it frozen in time—both me and the desk. For how long, I don't know, until EC came up behind me.

"Maddie."

I just sighed.

"Day-by-day…day-by-day…" EC's voice trailed off. "Come on. The meeting's about to start."

The scheduling bots had simply put the debriefing on my calendar, no invite to accept or decline. Just show up. Otherwise, I would have still been in bed, or in front of the tube in my bathrobe eating ice cream, or down at the bakery by my condo yielding helplessly to temptation.

I thought we'd be in the briefing room, but EC led me to a

small conference room on the tech side of the building. All the usual suspects were there: Bob and Puff and Q. EC sat down at the end of the table in the back of the room. I took the chair between him and Q, facing Bob and Puff. A moment later, Lt. Sands came in, closed the door, and sat down at the head of the table. I said a thankful prayer with my inside voice that the Captain wasn't going to be in the meeting.

"EC, how's Jake doing?" Sands asked, opening up his leather portfolio and pulling out some papers.

"He's still on the ventilator. His vitals are good. The docs hope to start bringing him out of the coma in the next couple of days." EC paused to wrestle his emotions back under control. I read the pain etched on his face, no doubt from the memories of his vigil at Patty's bedside and the battle lost after his wife's accident eighteen months ago. "Then, they'll get him moved to a step-down unit. Won't really know much more until he's conscious again."

"Good. Please keep me posted daily if you wouldn't mind."

"Will do."

Sands looked around the room at each of us. He pulled out his phone and showed us the screen as he powered it down. "No transcript here. We'll have *that* meeting in a day or two. Right now, I want to sort out exactly what we know; what we think we know; and what the hell is going on, before any, ah, upper echelon types start sticking their noses into our business. Everybody off now, please."

We all powered down our phones and put them in the center of the table.

Sands looked at Bob and Puff. "So, what do we know

about the bomb squad synthoid that went off the rails and attacked Jake?"

"Well, boy, I'll tell you, it's really something about that one," Bob said, adjusting his glasses. "Most of the chassis was intact and in good working order—though ten slugs in the cranium did some damage. Those BDU guys take really good care of their equipment, you know—not like the Streets Department and that sweeper in the garage—'cause, after all, their life depends on it. Firmware and software library updates and upgrades were up to snuff and properly logged. None of the hardware had been tampered with, so it was a completely remote takeover—and that's a real problem."

"Why's that?" Sands looked up from a note he was making.

"The Three Laws. They're for civilian units. Embedded on the boards in the BLC module." Puff's gravelly voice caught everyone by surprise. He rarely spoke more than a word or two during meetings. "Gotta be a hands-on job to hijack one of them. Gotta physically change out chip sets. Not so with government-issued units."

"Why not?"

"Well, see, use of force protocols are allowed in law enforcement and military droids," answered Bob. "Got to have 'em so they can do their jobs. Which means, if these guys figured out how to remote access one of our units…Well, that ain't good for nobody."

"How would they do it?"

"We got nothing. Nope, nothing at all out of the teardown. Nothing out of the ordinary in the droid's libraries or memory banks. Whatever was downloaded is vaporware now, or evaporated back up into the cloud."

Sands nodded his head and made a note. "I'll let you guys get back to the lab. Thanks."

"Okie-dokie."

Puff squinted at Lt. Sands. "This is serious bad mojo. *Serious.*"

Bob and Puff got up and left, closing the door behind them.

Lt. Sands looked at Q beside me. "Now, what about the server farm?"

"We got most of it intact. The bad guys tried but only managed to power down a couple of the units in the database tier, but it doesn't look like we lost any hardware and minimal data. I've got a half-dozen techs going through the millions upon millions of lines of code—and it keeps generating more on its own. Kind of crazy."

"The servers are still running?" EC asked. "What-the-what?"

"Observation is the best way to figure this thing out. Can't tell much about the habits of nocturnal creatures from staring at roadkill."

"So, how did they do this remote penetration of the droid that Puff was talking about?" Sands asked.

"Don't know yet. We didn't find any portal, either direct into the Grid via a secondary data link or into a transmission array to push into the white space." Q looked from Lt. Sands to EC and back to Sands. "Not to worry, guys. We've ensured that the thing is air gapped, so it's basically quarantined."

"So, you don't have anything yet, either." Sands looked at me and raised an eyebrow.

Q started to say something but thought the better of it. He shrugged his shoulders. Finally, he sighed, "We're working it. I mean it. The techs are putting in overtime."

"Then get back to it and let me know when you've made some progress."

Q sat back, stunned at being summarily dismissed from the meeting. He grabbed his phone and left, closing the door hard, but nowhere near what a hormonal teenage girl would.

"So, what's up, Lieu?" I asked.

"A little compartmentalization." Lt. Sands closed his portfolio, stood up, and walked down to our end of the table.

"You mean like a sinking ship?" EC asked.

"Eh…you guys know the interview drill. Divide and conquer."

"You don't think…" I didn't want to finish my thought.

Lt. Sands sat down across from me, folded his arms on the table, and leaned forward. "Look, Maddie, I have to ask: Do you want in on this? Sanchez and Jake and the whole 'Baron' thing—it's not a Robbery/Homicide gig. You know that, right? You'd have to be officially assigned to Artificial Crimes."

"A permanent transfer?" I asked.

"Doesn't have to be. A fill-in for Jake with EC, until…Or, if you'd rather, we could get you back into the rotation at your old desk upstairs pretty quick with a new partner and let ACU pursue the case. Your call. No harm, no foul, either way."

I didn't answer. I knew what Lt. Sands wanted to hear. And I knew what I would end up doing. I just didn't know if it was the right thing or not. I watched myself trace imaginary shapes on the tabletop in front of me, avoiding EC's stare. Jake would know the right thing to do, but he wasn't around to help me. "However long this takes, to see it through. To get these guys. I'll do it."

Lt. Sands sat back and smiled. "Good. 'Cause you two are the only ones I trust right now."

"Thanks, Maddie," EC whispered.

"Now, who is this Jamal guy and why did he kidnap that girl?"

Oh, my God. Amy! The pit of my stomach leapt and fell from somewhere high—I don't know where, but it was a long way down. I buried my head in my arms on the table. "How could I? How? Does he still have her?"

"Hard to tell, since she was already missing from the foster family," Lt. Sand said. "I saw the Amber Alert and your notes. I've got extra patrols cruising the Flats, keeping an eye out. Nothing so far."

"Q looked at the video loop on Jake's phone and thinks it was green screened with composite of the third floor and a live feed of the raid through the window," EC said. "Obviously, to draw Jake up into the ambush."

"And it worked. So, is this Jamal guy the Baron? Who the hell is he? And is he really a friend of Jake's?"

"He's an independent reporter who writes under the byline E.J. Quick," EC said. "Specializes in tech crimes—mostly white-collar stuff—so, of course, he's been a long-time fixture at the ACU. Latched on to Jake when he was first sent down. Don't know as I'd call them friends. They had a more of a *quid pro quo* kind of relationship, I'd say. Q has Samantha digging into his background."

"And why did he take this Amy girl? Who is she to him?"

"Jake and I grabbed her up at Jeffery's murder scene after you left. As a witness," I said. "Homeless kid who camps in the Flats. She eventually led us to the server farm building. I guess she came back home after she ran away from the foster family. I tried to tell that damn social worker—"

"Do you think he still has her now?"

I thought for a moment. "I hope not, but my heart tells me he does. It's leverage for him—over Jake…and me. I don't think he'd give that up. I don't think he's done with us."

"That's what I'm afraid of." Lt. Sand closed his portfolio. "Did we collar anyone of value the other night?"

"Some low level techie babysitters. And a bunch of homeless guys they let squat on the first floor as human camouflage. In case anyone came snooping around the building," EC answered. "The smell alone is enough to drive anyone off."

"Damn." Lt. Sands stood up. "Effective immediately, Maddie, you're working ACU. Don't wait for the paperwork. Just get after this guy and bring him down. Please get ahead of this before there's any talk of a task force—or calling in the Feds. Please."

I nodded.

"You." Lt. Sands pointed at EC, then at me as he said, "You take care of her."

"Will do."

With that, Lt. Sands left.

"Thanks, Maddie," EC whispered, even though we were the only ones left in the room.

This wasn't the career or the life or the future I had ever wanted…or even imagined.

I just buried my face in my hands, wishing I was home in my bathrobe eating ice cream.

~~~

The Invisible Mind

Criminals aren't the only ones who return to the scene of a crime.

The patrol officer posted at the building in the Flats recognized me and let me in without asking to see my badge. I went to the third floor first, unconsciously walking the path I had taken the morning of the raid in a much bigger hurry. Jake's blood was still on the floor and the filing cabinets. It gave me a chill. I saw small fragments of synthoid scattered around the spot where EC and I had put the robot down. Most of the big pieces had been taken into evidence for Bob and Puff. The floor was pock-marked where EC's shotgun blasts had shattered and severed the knee joints. There was a clean bullet hole up where its head had been. I guess I missed with one of my shots.

You bastard. I never did like that Jamal.

"Detective?" Q had come up close behind me while I was lost in thought.

"Jesus, Mother Mary. Don't do that. *Please.*"

"Sorry." Q stood beside me. "Is that Jake's blood?"

I nodded.

"I hate that guy."

I sighed. "Yeah, me too."

After an awkward silence, Q asked, "If I tell you something, you won't get mad, will you?"

Oh, God. Now what?

"I didn't really give Sands the full download on those servers in here—I mean, I did about what I know for sure, but maybe not what I suspect."

"And…"

"This guy Jamal? He's good. Damn good. Spooky good."

"Meaning?"

"This isn't just a server farm like typical infrastructure stuff for data storage, info access, automation, backbone or even pumping nefarious code through the Atlas Grid to the droids like we thought. Remember how I said it keeps generating code on its own?"

I nodded. There was something in Q's eyes as he spoke. Glassy and darting, they betrayed an admiring nervousness.

"You know, on the outer fringes of AI metaphysics—and mostly in the Darknet—there's talk of what it would take to control things, really control everything, like a system that not only moves information but creates it—No, more like creates a collective unconsciousness. An id, a digital id that moves people and events and societies in ways that no one knows is happening. You just wake up one day and the world is different, you are different—sometimes a little and sometimes a lot—because, well, you don't know why, just because. Because there's some, like, *invisible mind* at work. The possibilities, well, they're limitless."

"And that's what's downstairs? An invisible mind?"

"A serious attempt at it."

"And the murders?"

"Just a scratch on the surface."

~~~

The Baron

He savored the delectable irony of it all as he watched through the observation window in the Intensive Care Unit: Jake, the synthoid hunter, was being kept alive by machines.

Jamal, dressed in green surgical scrubs, pulled his phone out and tapped on the screen. Waitress Amy's head jerked around to the bed next to Jake's as the alarms on that patient's medical monitoring equipment began to flash and bleat.

"Code Blue to ICU bed nine," an emotionless automated voice announced over the public address system. Soon after the bed was swarmed by nurses and doctors.

Jamal did not wait to watch the patient die…

Thank you for reading my story.

About M.T. Bass

M.T. Bass lives, writes, flies and plays music in Mudcat Falls, USA.

www.MTBass.net

Available in Paperback & eBook

Artificial Intelligence? *Fuhgeddaboudit!*

Artificial Evil has a name…*Munchausen.*

When androids are reprogrammed into hit men, detectives of the Artificial Crimes Unit repo the AnSub and track down the hackers. Partners Jake and EC's case of an "extra-judicial" divorce settlement takes a nasty turn with DNA from a hundred-year-old murder in Boston and a signature that harkens back to the very first serial killer ever in London.

www.MTBass.net

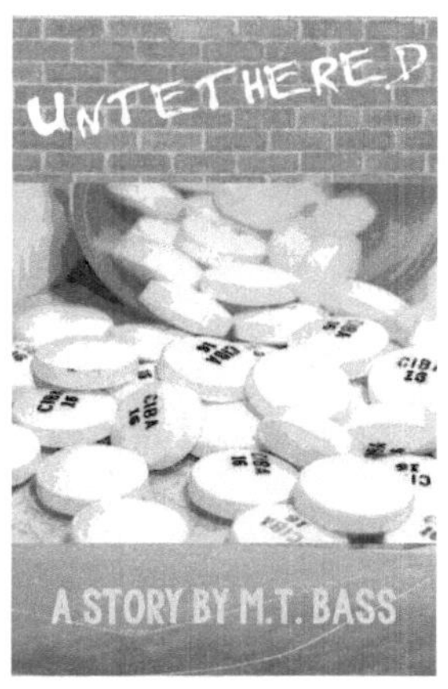

Available in eBook

At District High School #6241, Connor wants only to get close to Liz, the cheerleader whose locker is just across the hall, and forget the suicide of his father in jail, but his family's dark past and a rebellious nature force him to the fringes of student social circles and into an unlikely alliance to fight back against a tyranny of conformity.

www.MTBass.net

Available in Paperback & eBook

People ask me where I get the ideas for my books. In this case, I recall reading about Alaska bush pilots for fun. I must have watched *Animal House* and *Treasure of the Sierra Madre* around that time and…a few months later—Eureka! The words for the prologue and first chapter just started spilling out of my head. ("Clean up on aisle five.")

Seriously, what could go wrong? *Love & Betrayal…Murder & Mayhem…Friendship & Double-Crossing Partners in Pursuit of Buried Treasure…*

www.MTBass.net

Available in eBook

*Lodging — bending of the stalk of a plant (stalk lodging)
or the entire plant (root lodging)*

While World War II engulfs every nation on the globe, Rebecca and her high school friend Sarah can only dream of escaping a dreary, wind-blown existence in western Kansas, until their boring, stodgy old hometown fills with handsome young men learning to fly Army Air Corps bombers known as *Liberators*, and their lives are suddenly filled with temptation and, perhaps, true love.

www.MTBass.net

Available in Paperback & eBook

Kansas City, 1965 — Y.T. Erp, Jr. can't wait to leave for college at the University of California, Berkeley to escape not only the work, but especially all the phlegm-brained idiots at his father's aerospace company. Leaving behind a pregnant auburn-haired cheerleader, a sensuous red-headed siren plotting to usurp his familial ties, and his two best friends—one who ends up in Vietnam and the other in the Weather Underground—his "trip" on the wild side of the Generation Gap takes him from the psychedelic scene of Haight-Ashbury to the F.B.I.'s Ten Most Wanted list. Meanwhile, his father is consumed by the task of managing his unmanageable corporate team in the quest to help fulfill a President's challenge to "land a man on the moon."

www.MTBass.net

Available in eBook

Cleveland, 1977 — Grappling with a foreign policy crisis, the U.S. Government targets a hapless rock-'n'-roller as a Russian spy in a classic case of mistaken identity for an innocent, 'Wrong Man' hero…or *is he?*

Think of an unholy fictional union between the Rolling Stones and Alfred Hitchcock's *North by Northwest.*

Unlike any novel you have ever read, this one has a soundtrack. After all, a story whose characters are musicians should have…well…*music.* Right?

www.MTBass.net

Available in Paperback & eBook

Hollywood, 1950 — Former P-51 fighter pilot A. Gavin Byrd is on location for a movie shoot, when he gets a call from the police that his older brother, a prominent Beverly Hills plastic surgeon, has been found dead on his boat. The Lieutenant in charge of the investigation is ready to close the case as a suicide from the start, but "Hawk" doesn't buy it and decides to find out what really happened for himself.

With help from a former starlet ex-girlfriend, a friendly police sergeant whose life was saved in the war by his brother and a nosy Los Angeles Times reporter, Hawk's search for the truth takes him through cross-fire, dog fights and mine fields in Hollywood, Beverly Hills, Burbank and Las Vegas, and leads him into some of the darker corners of his brother's patient files and private life that he never knew existed.

www.MTBass.net

www.ingramcontent.com/pod-product-compliance
Lightning Source LLC
Chambersburg PA
CBHW060601190726
48283CB00003B/1111